The God Complex

Book Four of the Widow Maker Series

By:
Zoez Lajoune

D1666990

Cadmus Publishing
www.cadmuspublishing.com

Also by Zoez Lajoune

The Widow Maker Trilogy:
Book 1: The Awakening of The Widow Maker
Book 2: The Rise of The Widow Maker
Book 3: The Legend of The Widow Maker

Acknowledgements

I am forever grateful to all of you who have supported this unique storyline and believed in me as a writer. One who would not only tell an entertaining story, but that would share the truth about the things that we grapple with in the dark. To my publication's family at Cadmus Publishing. Thank you so much for giving me the opportunity to live out what so many dream they could do. Last and most importantly, to the One, whose grace and mercy lifts me, washes me, and sustains me. You are better to me than this old world could ever be. You are the True Vine and I Your branch. I write to serve Your purpose and to honor You first, Jesus.

Dedication

I dedicate this book to all of you who have struggled with various forms of mental health or who have been under the care of someone with mental health complexities. May you overcome the darkness and become the light.

CONTENTS

PROLOGUE

It is believed that true evil can be sensed by both dogs and children. That they can somehow see the stains permanently fastened to someone's soul. Like a hideous mark from the unforgettable choices of his past. Many whispers, below the watching eyes in storefront windows said, "He's the reason why all of the little one's cry and the dogs howl and bark every time that well-polished black, medical transport van pulled into town." Inside the privately owned van, immaculately dressed, was old Henry Lee Stonewall. He was on his way to his regularly scheduled physical therapy appointment.

Like an inkblot his mind would wonder "What do other's see when they look at me? Maybe they see me as the benevolent benefactor that I have been all these years to them? What about as an economic tyrant with the power to choke the life out of their community that is as fragile as the brittle bones in my arms? Perhaps they see me as just another free handout or nothing at all? Could it be that they see me like people once saw Ebenezer Scrooge and mumble 'Bah humbug' under their breath like bitter gall?" He was certain by the spite in their eyes that the latter was true for most of them.

As the last known living descendant of his family, he was the possessor of great wealth that few had ever known. He never felt he had reason to need anything or tried to win the social approval of anyone. It was purely because of the views of his new personal caretaker, Dr. Marcus Rutowski, that after two decades of isolation he began to venture outside of the Stonewall grounds to interact more with the public and live a well-balanced life. His life before was filled with loneliness and bitter memories, scarred by a childhood of unloving, cold, affectionless parents. Parents who kept a close watch day and night over the Stonewall Cotton Empire, begging in-laws, looking for handouts and several locked safes of jewels throughout the house.

As a young man some twenty plus years ago, he sought to fill his loneliness with prostitutes and wild parties until he met a young fair skinned colored girl half his age who stole his heart. Secretly they dated for a while until his parents found out and threatened to cut him off completely. The day she was about to tell him of her pregnancy he told her that he no longer wanted to be with her, that no woman was worth as much of his time that she had already taken up and the amount of money he spent constantly trying to impress her. Though being a simple girl, she never once asked him for anything.

That night while she lay in her bed and cried over him, her mother used what folk in the bayous call hoodoo to curse him. While he laid in bed between the drunken legs of a strange white woman that he had met outside a local boutique in town, he suffered a massive stroke that paralyzed the left side of his body, horribly slurred his speech, and left him confined to a wheelchair for the rest of his life. Now some fifteen years later as the lift in the van slowly lowered his wheelchair to the sidewalk a bitter look filled his eyes that reflected the iciness of his heart.

INTRODUCTION

s for the bayous they had always known a strange dryness. To the inhabitants it appeared as if The Lord God Himself had turned a blind eye to it. A longing sense of being forgotten lingered steadily in their eyes. Some believed that over several generations many of their lineages had become anchored to what folks over in the city of New Orleans called the badlands; a place where souls were destined in each generation to wander amongst the tombs of these savage parts as outcasts by society.

Only a few outsiders had ever grasped the scenic beauty that lay within its borders. A small group of annual snowbird residents even relished in the quietness that those born and bred there had grown to loath and despise. To them the quietness was soul drinking, unnerving, and possessive. For they knew of true darkness that lurked in the hills and had made its nesting ground at Stonewall Asylum. Some believed the darkness had been drawn there because of the history of other evil things that over decades lived on the grounds; obscure things that had all been tied to one family's societal vomit. Now that the door of fate was beginning to close on the soul of its last known living descendent, The Widow Maker had come to usher in a new era, to bring many of the very troubled souls their deliverance through the light of death. That by the sacrifices of the chose, this godforsaken wasteland of humanity may learn.

That for every door opened in the physical world one is also opened in the spirit realm. For every curse spoken a soul must also be sacrificed.

Part 1: Dark Reservations

CHAPTER 1
THE APPLICANT

The main house was sparsely lit with thin short candles. Electrical wiring was outdated in many rooms and had never been installed in some. A thick mildew scent crawled through the air that was repulsive and regurgitated. The interior design was marked by a forgotten era that predated the civil war. Neglect of the normal upkeep had left outdated newspapers, dirt caked dishes, soiled furnishings and worn-out area rugs pitched about the house. Nevaeh Sharai pinched her nose briefly under the mask of an itch as she and Dr. Rutowski stepped inside the foyer. A nurse practitioner from the Louisiana State Health Department greeted them from behind old Henry Lee Stonewall. As soon as he saw the beautiful young Nevaeh

Sharai he started smiling and ringing the help bell on his wheelchair. "Rr-ring, rr-rr-rr-rr-rr-ring" sounded the bell. "Sounds like you've made a new friend. I think he likes you" she said to Nevaeh. Then she leaned in over old man Stonewall's shoulder and said, "Don't you go cheating on me already. I thought I was your favorite."

Old man Stonewall smiled as he slowly looked up and past the starry, dark chocolate eyes of Nevaeh Sharai and to the face of Dr. Rutowski. Immediately his facial expression changed, and he became as silent as the wind that precedes a storm. A familiar dark aura shrouded Dr. Rutowski and engulfed the back of the foyer. Amidst the brief chilling encounter, she extended her hand to Nevaeh and said "Hi, I'm Heather Dubovich the state's nurse practitioner. I also oversee the home healthcare project across the southern district." "Nevaeh Sharai, the pleasure of your acquaintance is all mine," she said with a gorgeous smile. Nevaeh's light British accent took Heather a little by surprise at first when she introduced herself. 'How rare is it that she would be here in the bayous,' she thought. Still, bright and refreshing though with a hint of elegance which was definitely what Stonewall Plantation needed. The second introduction came formally "Um Ms. Dubovich, I'm Dr. Marcus…" She cut in like a giddy schoolgirl standing in front of her idol. "I know exactly who you are Dr. Rutowski. I graduated from the U of M back in Minnesota though up in Grand Rapids. Your lectures on rare case studies and the evolution of the human mind are taught across the state." Dr. Rutowski smiled and said "I'm impressed Ms. Dubovich. I see that you've done your homework. Heather continued, "I thoroughly research the background of every applicant that applies for a home healthcare position in my district. Normally I review an applicant's information, do a background check then schedule a telephone conference to discuss my findings. However, when I saw your application, I couldn't believe my eyes. I accepted you immediately and had to come in person to greet you with your first client. Still for the life of me I cannot understand why someone as qualified as you would apply for an entry level minimum wage position such as this."

Suddenly Dr. Rutowski began to hear the familiar chime of six nickels falling to the ground as his vision grew hazy. He braced himself as the methodical soul consuming voice of the Widow Maker whispered to him, "Careful doctor what you tell her. Less Ms. Hatchfield finds herself sharing that box with a guest upstairs in the attic." A piercing stare followed by Dr. Rutowski's calculated response in a deescalating tone offered "I do understand that I may appear to be overqualified for this position but isn't our goal to provide the highest possible form of personalized care to those in need. Plus, I've given careful consideration to moving my private practice to the bayou area, for personal health purposes. To stop punishing my body winter after winter during the harsh elements of the Twin Cities. Plus, from what I hear these bayous are ravaged with strange customs and mental health complexities. They show much promise for advanced research and dire need for unorthodox psychiatric therapy. I figured that this position would give me firsthand information on what types of unmet needs are present. So that I may develop a good ground game plan before officially offering fulltime psychiatric services to those in remote areas like this. Those who can't afford to travel to big cities like Baton Rouge or New Orleans for that matter. Trust me Ms. Dubovich this position, although very important, will be a temporary one. Once I've acquired the necessary data and adjusted to the culture. I'll be turning the position back over to your very capable hands. However, we can cross that bridge when the time comes. Now if you're still willing to have me where shall we begin?"

Heather stepped to the side and gestured with a smile, "This here is Mr. Henry Lee Stonewall. He was the first patient to be enrolled in our statewide home healthcare program. No patient has been with us longer. It's through his numerous and most generous donations that we were able to expand our home healthcare program into the bayou area and provide private medical transport to many in need in these parts. So, he's a very big deal to us." Nevaeh Sharai smiled as she rang his help bell. Then kneeled to his eyelevel and introduced herself. "I see you don't talk much. That's okay I like quiet company. How about you ring your help bell three times when you're trying to get my attention in specific? I think we're going to get along just fine," she finished as she stood back up.

Dr. Rutowski stepped forward and said, "Mr. Stonewall, may I call you Henry?" One ring of the bell sounded in yes as a response to his question. I'm going to be your new personal caretaker. I want to assure you that I will do all I can to help you obtain a better quality of life. I know from years of practice that sometimes wheelchair bound patients may suffer neglect. Ms. Sharai and I believe in the highest possible form of care covering everything from personal hygiene to recreational activities. I'm sorry that your last caretaker abandoned you. I do understand that you and Ms. Hatchfield were close. It is for that reason, why I will respect the personal box that she is in."

Heather thought it quite strange how he spoke about the disappearance of Ms. Hatchfield. To her recollection she had never once mentioned Ms. Hatchfield during her brief introduction. She also wondered how he knew they were close. Dr. Rutowski continued as he stepped gracefully behind old man Stonewall, slowly turned his wheelchair, and proceeded to push him back into the living room. "Over the course of time I hope that I can gain your trust by giving you proper care to regain some basic motor skills and help you overcome any personal obstacles you may have," he concluded. Nevaeh Sharai stopped dead in her tracks once she was able to survey the layout of the first floor.

Had it not been for her loyalty to Dr. Rutowski she

would not have pulled her travel bag another foot. Heather politely said, "I do not recall if I posted in the electronic file, I forwarded to you about Mr. Stonewall that this position requires an onsite caretaker overseeing management of the entire grounds. You would be granted limited power of attorney with access to a sizeable grant of which you may use for a wide range of purposes. Such as contracting grounds workers to whip this place into shape. So, you could indeed make some significant changes around here to the décor in both style and scheme. Now if you will follow me, I'll show you to your private quarters. Although keep in mind you will have the ability to relocate and modify as you see fit." As soon as Ms. Dubovich handed Dr. Rutowski the keys to the grounds he handed them over to Nevaeh Sharai. He draped a clean woolen blanket across the shoulders of the old man and whispered into his ear, "How about you show me these historic grounds you have here."

Halfway down the hall Dr. Rutowski spoke over his shoulder, "Ms. Dubovich it was very nice to meet you. Nevaeh after you see Ms. Dubovich out can you please prepare some chamomile tea?" Heather smiled and said, "Have a good day Dr. Rutowski, it was delightful to meet you."

Over the squeak of the wheels from old man Stonewall's chair Dr. Rutowski replied, "The pleasure was all mine. Please inform Nevaeh of everything that we need to know about the grounds of Stonewall

Plantation and spare no detail. You will find that Ms. Sharai has a knack for retaining unusually high amounts of data." It was then that Heather understood Nevaeh Sharai was not only Dr. Rutowski's personal assistant but was also a rare case study of his.

Sleet rain rapped against the bay window that overlooked raging waters blanketed by a closing storm front. The squeak of the wheelchair dissipated as the wheels rolled to a stop. Suddenly Dr. Rutowski began to hear the familiar chime of six nickels falling to the ground as his vision grew hazy. It was then that the old man Stonewall saw the reflection of the Widow Maker standing over him through a flickering cast of storm lightning in the window. Upon hearing the help bell on his wheelchair ring three times Nevaeh looked eerily down the hall. Quickly she said to Ms. Dubovich, "I have an awful lot to prepare. Can we continue this discussion some other time, perhaps over tea?" Heather responded, "Sure, I'll call you later in the week to schedule something." Then she proceeded towards the door. As soon as the door to the foyer was closed Nevaeh briskly walked down the hall towards the continued ringing of the help bell on old man Stonewall's wheelchair.

The Widow Maker stared piercingly through the reflective barrier of the window and down at the frightened old man. Then he twisted a dark tale and said, "Twas the night before damnation when all through the graveyard every eyeball was crying and nose dripping snot. The souls waited by their tombstones in chilling despair. They knew that The Light of Death would come and behold I am here." Terrified old man Stonewall mumbled and rang his help bell all the more as Nevaeh Sharai quickened her pace down the hall. The Widow Maker leaned in closely and whispered in his ear while watching her approach, "Calm yourself old man before I'm moved to reunite you with your family legacy outside in that convenient little burial plot."

Immediately upon hearing his fate the old man mumbled nothing else. His finger slowed to a twitch and rested softly beside the bell. Thoughts of Ms. Hatchfield and the sound her head made when it struck the trunk in the middle of the floor. The crack of her vertebrae as the metal leg brace separated cartilage and spine. It all crossed the Widow Maker's mind as his grip tightened on the chair. Nevaeh, who knew all too well the heinous things the Widow Maker was capable of, wisely, yet cautiously said, "Pardon me Dr. Rutowski, I've seen Ms. Dubovich out. She will be calling later in the week to schedule a time to stop by next to see how we've settled in. I'm going to go and prepare some chamomile tea for you now. Will you need anything else at this moment?" When Dr. Rutowski turned toward her to respond she noticed the cosmic electrical flashes in his eyes and knew that like Dr. Jekyll, who was scourged by the spirit of Mr. Hyde. That darkness had consumed him yet again. The Widow Maker spoke through his teeth, "No that will be all for now."

The old man peeked at her out of the corner of his eye with a look that told her he understood a dark, disturbed and very dangerous presence was there. Since Dr. Rutowski mentioned the possibility of moving his private practice to the bayou area of New Orleans, Louisiana, she had wondered what provoked him to pick this is place. Based off the look in old Henry Lee Stonewall's eyes she knew that this place was at the center of his decision and not by happenstance. That he had somehow engineered this whole encounter with Henry Lee Stonewall for a dark purpose. Subtly she extended her hands toward the handles of the wheelchair and said, "How about I take this one with me for company while you tour the grounds and decide on sleeping arrangements."

CHAPTER 2
THE WILL OF THE DEAD

————◦○⟨≈⟩○◦————

It was not long after their transition that the Widow Maker proceeded to lend his expertise toward rapid deterioration of old man Stonewall's health. He kept Nevaeh Sharai distracted with management of the entire grounds and oversight of his specifications toward renovations. Day by day Dr. Rutowski skillfully traded two opposing masks. Publicly with Mr. Stonewall he portrayed himself as invested, attentive to every little need of his and even a bit fussy over him at times with a watchful parental eye. However, when they were alone his visage quickly changed and he would perform many unspeakable malicious acts upon him. First, he disarmed the help bell on his wheelchair so that he could not call Nevaeh Sharai for assistance. Then on numerous cool and stormy nights after bath time he often left him half naked and wet by the open patio doors. Meanwhile, he sat with his back to him by the warmth of the fireplace. On several occasions Nevaeh Sharai found him sitting alone in the kitchen inhaling the toxic fumes of a turned-on unlit oven. Once she went to check on him in the middle of the night and found him out on the front lawn. As she approached from behind through the sleet rain, she could hear a faint whisper from the frightened old man of "Rrr-rrr." When she asked him why he did not ring his help bell for her the old man tapped the handle of his chair while he stared petrified at her. Through slow desperate spurts he continued to try to imitate the sound of the help bell. Slowly she looked down through the harsh slap of sleet rain upon her face and discovered that the bell had been hammered and crushed on his chair by some sort of pipe wrench.

Her constant interference reluctantly moved the Widow Maker to relent from his methodical torture of the old man for a season to prevent from having to lift the head of Dr. Rutowski's bothersome assistant from off her body. Being naïve to the depth of the mind games the Widow Maker was apt to play. Over time it appeared to her that he had actually forsook his dark side obsession with killing the old man. That instead the good doctor's attention had become centered around thoughts of expanding his case load and offering group therapy on the newly renovated rounds. Subsequently Nevaeh's protective watch grew more and more lax as she settled into her growing role as the head groundskeeper.

Meanwhile the daytime treatment staff grew swiftly as Dr. Rutowski's vision came to fruition. With this came the need for additional licensing and department aids of which Dr. Rutowski was able to secure due to his many outstanding credentials. Out of the candidates that applied for these new positions the Widow Maker moved Dr. Rutowski to select sketchy individuals who did not belong working in the mental health field. Individuals that had been red flagged by the state's review board for various flagrant incidents involving patient care. His dark psychosis targeted a list of these individuals under the guise of wanting to give a deserving few a second change. By helping them to learn to live above the demons they could never escape. It was these individuals who had found themselves victims of their own unfortunate life circumstances. Like a skillful spider the Widow Maker lured them into his deadly web that camouflaged himself.

One applicant was a single parent mother that had been criminally charged with neglect of her autistic son. Her file indicated that she left her only child behind in an unsafe environment, her trailer park home. In her own defense she stated that she had fled from there in the middle of an assault to call authorities on her physically abusive spouse. Dr. Rutowski appointed her as head of his residential care staff.

Case by case Dr. Rutowski built his staff from the

germ-infested petri dish of those who would simply do their eight-hour shift and go home. People so grateful to be back working in healthcare that fear of losing their jobs would cause them to swiftly turn a blind eye to any questionable healthcare practices. Once the grounds were strategically staffed for additional residential care Dr. Rutowski added biweekly impatient group therapy sessions to his caseload. This was in addition to performing court ordered evaluations.

It was not long after that the Widow Maker took the old man out to the woodshed. There he severed his head with an axe. He placed six highly polished nickels into his bulging eyes as a fee for The Boatman, set his head on a freshly chopped pile of pine wood and left. But not until he had Dr. Rutowski forge a living will that gave him full endowment of the Stonewall estate. The last legal act of old man Stonewall was done as he placed his fingerprint on the document. The act served in the same manner authoritatively that it had done for at least fifteen years as his signature. The document had been officiated in estate court just three weeks prior to his untimely demise. Throughout his life he had been called a fifth-generation slave trader. He was a shrewd ungodly man who sued several local charities for violations of their lease agreements.

When around Christmastime they had opened the doors of their local nonprofit businesses to shelter the homeless from the cold, the front page of the local newspaper, which was also owned by the Stonewall

Estate, had listed his death as a "Tragic assault on humanity by an unidentified intruder on the Stonewall grounds." At the funeral, which was open to the public and held next to the old family burial lot on the Stonewall grounds, several long blasts from a warning alarm blared out across the bayous signifying that as one era had come to an end. The commencement of a new era was beginning through the baptism of a purge. In a statement to the press Dr. Rutowski spoke eloquently about the rich heritage of the Stonewall generations. How many of their contributions greatly benefited the community? That those efforts would continue under his leadership, expand into new horizons, and meet the ever-changing needs of the bayous. To win the hearts of the people he announced the historic grounds opened to the public for psychiatric services as the new Stonewall Asylum.

Within the confines of the asylum walls Dr. Rutowski placed a secure patient wing, one by which he housed and treated those that had a broad spectrum of antisocial derangements, schizoaffective disorders marked by unusual acute episodes of schizophrenia with clinical depression. That spawned family isolation and made them social outcasts in society. Out of the twelve patients in Dr. Rutowski's group, three of them required meal restrictions such as paper plates, Dixie cups, thin plastic utensils and no meat with large bones in it. Large bones could potentially be used as weapons.

Everyone that was housed on the secure wing

of Stonewall Asylum was restricted to no physical contacts during visits. They were, however, permitted a quick closely monitored handshake and or hug at the beginning and end of each visit. Patient's rooms were inspected daily. Approved clothing consisted of a two-piece hospital scrub uniform without pockets. Shoes were not permitted at any time. For security purposes, only electronic mail skim read by staff was allowed from immediate family members.

These measures were particularly important for Raquel. Her psychosis led her to believe that she had been sent back in time by an angel to be God's judgement, to close a local grocery store that she claimed was a front for local gang activity. The police responded to the store location after several shots were reported fired there. Inside they found a nineteen-year-old store clerk dead at the cash register. He was slumped over an acceptance letter in his right hand for an athletic scholarship to the University of Mississippi, Ole Miss. After further search of the store Raquel was found. She had crouched naked behind the meat counter and written several strange symbols on the glass window with blood from raw meats inside the cooler. Still, in reality she was a forty-five-year-old grandmother whose mind snapped once she learned that her 20-year-old daughter and newborn grandbaby were killed by crossfire shooting between two local gangs. When they were found the child's mother was balled up underneath the open back door to the car, next to the curb, in front of Raquel's house.

Her daughter's back had been riddled by bullets. A single shot to the abdomen ended the small child's life. When Raquel finally broke through the crowd and saw them, she let out a soul wrenching scream. Desperately she held both of them in her arms and cried while she rocked back and forth. The veil of her heart rent from top to bottom and exposed the anguish of her soul. She repeatedly cried out "Dear God no! No God, please no!" until the paramedics arrived. Not long after her loved ones were pronounced dead. Raquel's mind blacked out in pure rage. Later that night she went to the corner store still covered in their blood looking for retribution. Now she stood and whispered strange things to the wall, under her breath. Daily she plotted and planned to escape the asylum so that she could go and finish what she had started.

Then there was Emily who believed she had been physically cursed due to her mother's promiscuous ways during her pregnancy. Her only desire was to see the world that had been so cruel to her since birth, burn with all its perfection. Her psychological niche caused her to readily display a theatrical performance of helplessness due to her Down's syndrome. Little did an unsuspecting few know that she was actually a very clever woman whose physical appearance did no justice to reveal the level of intellect that she actually possessed. Craftily she baited gullible humanitarians through this cloak to befriend them, to manipulate them and eventually to kill them.

Out of the twelve patients in Dr. Rutowski's impatient group there was one patient however, that did not mesh with the others. He often appeared quiet, reserved, and emotionally separated from the normal mental dross of frustrations and complaints. That surface because of the intense heat inside the therapeutic caldron of Stonewall Asylum. Most of the group believed that the main reason it was so hard for Sam Green to relate to the rest of them was the fact that he was an ex-cop. One who had never known the hard knock side of life that many of them had tried desperately to claw themselves out of. Lives full of abandonment, addiction, prostitution, physical abuse, mental cruelty, and social acceptability to poverty as long as narcotics were present. In addition to being an ex-cop Sam Green served as a volunteer firefighter. Prior to that he served two tours in Iraq and was a highly decorated Marine with metals of valor. He was the loving father of a 4-year-old son with leukemia. His wife, Rene, worked in law enforcement as a 911 dispatch operator. They faithfully attended Sunday Church service at the local parish and spent countless hours as fundraisers for St. Jude's Children's Research Hospital.

The prosecution argued in court that he was completely sane and that his actions were those of a man under extreme financial duress. That after he depleted all his military savings and borrowed against his pension several times to cover the high cost of medicine for his son's disease and procedures that his health insurer would not cover. They claim he maliciously shot the mother with child at night during their bedtime story. To put an end to his bills and cash in on a $50,000 life insurance policy.

The defense argued that Sam Green loved his family and suffered horribly from PTSD. That while sleepwalking after having went to bed early, he found himself in the midst of a horrifying night terror, of which he had only partially awakened. He was pinned down under enemy gunfire in Iraq. He crawled into the hall, broke the glass casing on the cabinet, secured the rifle, a box of shells and proceeded to crawl half delusional into the living room. Upon seeing the enemy instead of his wife, holding a firearm to the head of his son, he quickly loaded and fired the weapon. The single shot from a 302-rifle travelled with such velocity that when it struck the back of the book it feathered several pages. The force of the projectile collapsed the chest of the child, snapped the breastbone of the mother, and spouted blood-soaked cotton as the bullet exited the back of the chair and lodged into the wall.

CHAPTER 3
WINDING STAIRCASES

T here were many dark secrets to be unearthed across the grounds of Stonewall Asylum. This was in part because the current house had been rebuilt from the ground up over its preexisting foundation. This, like so many others, had been ransacked by Union troops then set ablaze by fire and destroyed during the liberation of the South. Unfortunately, physical civil liberties can never truly liberate people's minds, only Christ can do that. Therefore, it was not long after those Union troops left that a new form of slavery took root like a vicious weed. It unmercifully choked the life out of all the beautiful fruit that many had envisioned that the South would produce.

Consequently, it enslaved scores of people in their thinking with paralyzing false ideologies about life. It was then that many people fled to New York behind whispers of an economic boom. At that time Stonewall Plantation expanded from the ashes of a lack of competition in the South, becoming the nation's top cotton manufacturer and amassed a small fortune. Still no matter how much drywall anybody ever tried to hang up there or fresh coats of paint they slapped on to try to conceal the roots of Stonewall Asylum, there would always be some trace of the original grounds left. Dual hidden passageways within the walls ran parallel to the main corridors. Observation rooms were cloaked behind bookshelves to provide the perfect opportunity to divine the true intent of one's heart.

Daily as the construction crew worked out the intricate designs of Dr. Rutowski they discovered many evidences of human atrocities in various places about the grounds. Some of these locations required meticulous excavation to preserve civil war era artifacts and document findings. As reconstruction drew to a close the general contractor ran into an obstruction that halted the final leveling of the main building's foundation. A condemned aqueduct made of an old collapsed drainpipe served as the only access point to an unknown condemned basement area two stories beneath the newly renovated administration wing of the asylum. According to the original blueprints of the grounds the area did not even exist.

Dr. Rutowski intercepted the general contractor while he was on his way to reveal the discovery to

Nevaeh Sharai. When he learned of the find he went to investigate it himself. A camera with a high-powered lens and LED light was attached to a remote-control voyager and sent down the aqueduct to reveal exactly what they were dealing with. There was darkness down there that literally swallowed the LED light. Just beyond the aqueduct was the old house slave's quarters, a laundry room, an old incinerator room and what appeared to be some type of operation room with medieval contraptions. The construction consisted of Oval shaped limestone sealed with brick mortar made of mud and straw. Bars made of tempered iron secured each cavernous entrance. Sets of broken rusted shackles were draped over old torch post. A large, jagged knife made from the jawbone of a donkey with swaddling cloth wrapped around one end like a handle lay discarded on an old Gurney with dried blood and small chunks of blackened human flesh embedded between the teeth.

While doctor Rutkowski carefully examined the video footage the general contractor rattled some design options for the area. He quickly removed the pencil from behind his ear and sketched on the wall three possible access points of staircases leading down from outside on the lawn. He rattled off the necessity of installing an additional support beam for the chamber and a ventilation window for the incinerator room. Meanwhile, Dr. Rutkowski had already begun to hear the familiar chime of six nickels falling to the ground as his vision grew hazy. The Widow Maker scoffed unsavorily at the contractor's myopic opinion and said, "Unlike the rest of the grounds I will personally oversee the transformation of this site. I also prefer that this matter be kept confidential even from the groundskeeper Ms. Sharai since her department is primarily in dealing with the oversight of the general grounds and physical care. My vision for this area is that it will contain the most sensitive information on grounds. You say that it was not listed on the previous floor plan? Let's leave it off this one as well and list the renovation costs on a separate invoice from the other labor cost. I would like for an access point be made available by winding staircase from my office only so that I may also use this chamber as a restricted area for personal research of sedatives and hypnotic therapy sessions for my most disturbed patients. One whose violent outburst and behavioral tendencies would only serve to incite the emotional instability of the other patients. For now, have the area cleaned out and work on some plans to install the winding staircase from my office. Which, I believe…" He paused and recalled by memory seeing the end of that same aqueduct protruding from the ground beneath is office window while he sat at his desk one afternoon reading from the journal that he had received from Carlos MacIntyre.

After a moment's pause the Widow Maker continued and said, "The bookcase in my office should suffice. Perhaps even use it as a covering to cloak the staircase for extra security?" with a rather smug look on his face the contractor said, "I've always wanted to do a project like this." The Widow Maker stepped uncomfortably close to him and nearly placed his lips on the contractor's earlobe. Then as he pulled a highly polished nickel from out of his pocket and proceeded to roll it down the miniature staircase of his knuckles over and over again, he measured his next words carefully and said, "Don't remove too much of the primitive décor. I'd hate to ruin the callous look. For let's face it, after you strip away the fancy suit and tie along with all the etiquette phrases and cordial responses rendered suffocatingly over the impulses of the flesh. Mankind is at best," he paused and adjusted the contractor's tie then concluded in a hateful tone, "undeniably primitive."

The general contractor swallowed slow and hard as Dr. Rutowski turned and walked off. After he took a couple of steps he paused and looked chillingly over his shoulder at him then said, "By the way, once you gain entry to the chamber gather those shackles along with that blade made from the jawbone of an ass into a box and bring them to me. I believe they will make excellent additions to my gallery. For each already has its own heart wrenching stories to tell of hellish psychological tortures, physical cruelties and human atrocities." The general contractor stood there in total shock completely dumbfounded by what he had just heard. Meanwhile, the hustle and bustle of the construction crew carried on around them. The Widow Maker looked back over his shoulder at him as if he could somehow sense his anxiety building within him from an apprehension of evil. With a chilling gaze underscored by a malicious smile he said, "The better judgement you seek is evidence of what you still lack. Shall I contract someone else to accomplish this simple task or can you manage?"

The general contractor thought quickly about all the money he was making off this job and how it would not hurt to put away a little extra off the books for a family vacation. He shook himself as if from a trance and mumbled, "No, no I'll see to it myself." The Widow Maker slowly turned his head back towards the excavated hallway. While he made his exit he extended him an invitation, "Should you make any other noteworthy discoveries I will be in my office. I do expect to see you with that little box sometime between lunch and dinner." The contractor asked absent mindedly, "Which room did you settle on again for your office?" The Widow Maker seethed in a low annoyed tone, "I just told you absent minded little monkey." Then with a mock smile on his face he said "Our office is directly above that chamber you showed us, and I'd really like for you to stop by. We can show you the bookshelf those stairs will work excellent behind and of course hear your plans on removing the portion of that aqueduct protruding from under our window. If by chanced we're out just leave the box on our desk." He smiled at him hungrily, turned and walked off.

The contractor thought it was very strange how Dr. Rutowski spoke of himself as we. His dark gaze fell on the general contractor again while he waved bye to him with a pinky finger until both of his eyes passed the corner of the wall. Something told the contractor that if he delivered that box, it would be the last box he ever delivered.

Out front a costal moving truck slowly wound its way up the driveway to deliver the last remaining office furniture and therapeutic aid items to Dr. Rutowski from the University of Minnesota campus in downtown Minneapolis. While Nevaeh Sharai emerged on the deck platform and waved to the guard booth to let the truck through the secure gate. Dr. Rutowski stood and watched from a window in the lobby as the truck unloaded. Repeatedly he checked his watch until he noticed a small white van winding its way up the old gravel road. Nevaeh was quite aware of his presence in the lobby's window. When she turned to gesture to him that she did not know why this second van was there he was gone and all she saw was the curtain swaying. She assumed that he probably went to go prepare for his next group. Not being privy of any additional deliveries to be received that day, she headed out to the gate to learn the contents the van did carry. When she made her way around the curve of the driveway to the guard booth. Dr. Rutowski quickly cried after her from behind while he made his way across the grass to intercept her before she reached the gate. He said "I'll tend to this delivery since it's only a small package of modules to aid me in my personal research. How about you go and relax a little bit." Nevaeh protested "Who shall attend to the log?"

Dr. Rutowski stopped dead in his tracks as he began to hear the familiar chime of six nickels falling to the ground as his vision grew hazy. The Widow Maker seethed at her, "We will manage quite well. It would be wise for you to check in on some of the other clients on the secure impatient wing. They, unlike you, don't enjoy great privileges about these grounds." Which was his way of saying do not forget that you are still first our patient and second our assistant. She had been brought here from the United Kingdom on a temporary visa to assist Dr. Rutowski in a controlled experiment, to test the limits of her rare ability to recall highly vivid details about persons, places, or things. However, at any given time with the stroke of his pen that could all change. She could be terminated from her position as his assistant and updated to the impatient client list. The second possible outcome would deliver an even more shrewd fate for her. If the case study were to be rendered complete. She would be immediately returned to the travesty of life she was found in. A life to where she struggled to survive in the Red-Light District of Amsterdam as a low-grade prostitute.

Nevaeh smiled politely and said, "Very well, by the time you're done here there will be a fresh setting of chamomile tea waiting for you in your office." As she headed back up the stairs to the main entrance doors she glanced back over her shoulder. Her eyes quickly and carefully studied the scene of Dr. Rutowski with the delivery truck driver. First, the eagerness on Dr. Rutowski's face as the driver eased him the box. Second, the gestures that clearly showed the level of fear in the driver's mind that said he prayed that he would not drop that box and it somehow came open. Low under her breath Nevaeh mumbled to herself, "I know that you're trying to hide something from me. I'm going to find out just what is in that little unmarked package you're signing for that didn't it show up on my log?"

That evening Nevaeh Sharai stood with the general contractor and looked over the intricate designs of Dr. Rutowski. That had been skillfully applied to the only access corridor that led from the secure impatient wing of the asylum to the main entrance public lobby. The complete path of the corridor turned in a 360-degree counterclockwise direction. The walls were seamless. Strategically it contained twenty-eight doors with no visible doorknobs or handles on them. There were no signs, markers or names present to signify which door led to which place. The hallways, though short, appeared to be long like the mind puzzle effect that is created by a blend of optical similarity in high security federal buildings like the United States Marshall's Office. Special groves carved into the doors assisted to pull them open. There were seven doors in each hall. Three doors were evenly spread across all the walls on the left from corner to corner. While there were four doors evenly spread across all the walls on the right from corner to corner so that looking down each hall it visually appeared an endless rotating maze of duplicate doors.

All of this was done to confuse anyone that may have somehow evaded the watchmen at the guard's station then tried to escape the asylum through the public lounge area. Patients reasoned that the lobby door would be in front of them at the far end of the hall. Usually, the mind depicts that to flee and escape something one must run in a straight path away from it. The farther you can see it behind you the closer you are to freedom. This panic induced lie would never prove successful for anyone seeking to escape Stonewall Asylum. The patients did not know that the door to their freedom was actually the first door in the hall on the left.

CHAPTER 4
CRADLED DREAMS

—◦◦◦—

While the orderlies closed the common areas and gathered several of the patients from their rooms in preparation for the evening group, Dr. Rutowski sat quietly by, mentally detached in a trance, and listened to the sound of the storm that grew steadily outside. Carefully he studied the demeanor of the patients from a strategically positioned chair by a window until the remaining chairs were filled. His face was concealed by the looming shadow underneath the dim light of the inverted shade of a lampstand in the corner. Light receded from the pupils of his eyes as they grew dim and barely visible at times, like the transition of the sun, through the trees of a forest, across a lake at dusk. As if entranced by the sound and sway of the arm of the rocking ticker that sat on his desk, which he regularly used to place his patients under hypnosis so that he could easily explore the dark chambers of their minds. Slowly his conscious mind drifted behind the rhythmic taps of the sleet rain upon the window. Periodically when he spoke to steer the night's conversation his voice was low, intuitive, and crisp. A candlelike flame flickered in his eyes each time he was abducted from the soothing rumble of the storm that persisted outside. In that moment, his mental awareness shifted to the mindless banter being mumbled by several of his clients at the table. When the moment passed his conscious mind retracted and recoiled much tighter. He sat and engaged with the group completely unaware that his subconscious mind steadily relinquished its control to the possessive sway of another Egyptian Blackness.

While he spoke to the group the Widow Maker subdued control over one-half of his body, guided his hand and wrote on the notepad on his lap. There from his seated position he said, "At this time I would like to bring tonight's group to order." Everyone grew quiet as the last patient took his seat. Dr. Rutowski continued, "Before I present tonight's topic, I have an announcement. In order to give you the highest possible form of personalized care I am going to modify our regular group meetings. Starting next week, we will no longer meet on Tuesdays and Thursdays after dinner. Scheduled recreational activities will continue on the weekends depending on staff and availability."

The group began to cheer and discuss different activities they wanted to do on nights off. Dr. Rutowski interrupted, "Hold on, hold on, there's more. My intent is to allow you the opportunity to better process intense group discussions we have so that you may absorb more of the therapy offered. Lastly, I will be moving our twenty-minute individual check-in sessions from Monday, Wednesday and Friday mornings to the Tuesday and Thursday time slots. I will meet with six of you on Tuesday and the other six on Thursday."

While the group never really gave it any thought as to why these night sessions needed to be added so abruptly, Lorraine, the head of the residential care staff eyed him curiously. In the past she had worked under psychiatrists who gradually adjusted a patient's treatment plan over the course of several weeks. For decades this had been the common universal psychiatric approach. This method allowed the patient time to incrementally adjust to new schedules, routines, and treatment concepts. This method also decreased the likelihood of behavioral setbacks and the need for additional medications in order to cope. Since she had never seen a psychiatrist do a complete shift in treatment approach, she thought it was quite strange. Her suspicions grew quietly within her as to why the sudden change in patient care for the entire group. She was very grateful for her job and would not dare question him in public. So, from that time on she purposed to find an opportune time to speak to him privately in his office.

The most destructive acts of deception ever portrayed were always embedded in half-truths of obtaining a better life. They quickly offered some reflective revelation on how this new approach to life would bring greater success and that the person without it was being unjustly mistreated. Time and time again snice the Garden of Eden no matter who played the role of the deceiver, the end result has always been the same. The sword of truth delivered three devastating blows that became a painful epitaph for whoever ate the fruit of the lie. They never got what was promised, they soon after regretted it and in the end, they paid a terrible price.

It was not too long after that the night's topic was underway that Emily, the Down Syndrome Killer, theatrical performance of helplessness to covet attention was in full swing. She pretended as if she could not read any of the handouts. Then like out of a movie her face became like porcelain and she instantly adorned a frightful look. Next, she signaled under the table for a residential aid that stood nearby. Dr. Rutowski watched her carefully as the orderly approached. Once close she whispered to him, "I don't feel safe. Can you help me find my room?" Captivated by her plea he felt gullible like so many of her victims had to her request. He extended his hand to her. Other patients watched them out of the corner of their eyes as she reached out slowly with a shaking hand. Being privy to the games she played, Dr. Rutowski said, "Emily, if you aren't able to stay in group with your peers, I will need to have a one-on-one session with you tonight before I leave to keep you up to speed with the rest of the group. It would be counterproductive if you fell behind." He passed and looked at the rest of the patients one-by-one in their eyes. He did this to underscore a fine point for all of them that if they were not happy at Stonewall Asylum and thought they either deserved or was able to manipulate preferential treatment so they could undermine him at any given turn, think again. His voice was kind and soft, although his eyes burned with contempt. His eyes slowly passed each face until his gaze firmly rested back on Emily. He continued, "It would be most unfortunate for any of you if I could not somehow accommodate your treatment needs. I would be left with no choice except to turn your care over to the Department of Corrections. The living conditions lack some things to be desired. Still, they have a far wider range of staff resourced than we do at this small facility. Emily sensed that she had been backed into a corner. Knowing it was best to take her wounded ego and retreat into humility she faked a dry cough twice and asked for some water. The orderly standing nearby poured her some. Immediately after she drank it, she said, "Oh that was refreshing. I think I'm ok to stay in group for the night." Dr. Rutowski shot a testing smile at the group and said, "Excellent, let's continue."

Within three months' time all the internal and external renovations were complete. City council members as well as the state medical licensing board came to tour the grounds of the asylum and marveled at its genius. Dr. Rutowski stood in front of a podium in a small conference room and spoke eloquently. He smiled smugly and addressed every question with great details. How he had taken all the unlikely ingredients of a psychiatric cake mix; the patient's hopes, regrets, humor, psychosis, health, and trauma. He treated all these substances like the individual ingredients of the natural cake mix. Naturally, some of these things, when sampled individually, were not that appealing. It was the same in the mind of Dr. Rutowski. Howbeit once he had carefully organized and delicately balanced all these things over time, he was able to bring forth this sweet savory cake that now stood in front of their eyes. His explanation of protocols and day to day operations removed all their doubts as to the facility's security measures put in place as a safeguard for the community. That after decades of being classified as a remote area marked by abandoned ideas and people lost within themselves.

They finally had a respectable noteworthy facility overseen by a highly respected physician. A place that he expected to be both supported and protected at all costs. Little did they know that hidden beneath the highly polished floors, executive furniture and modern look of an upscale treatment facility that closely resembled more of a therapeutic span than the likes of any typical asylum. The true Stonewall Asylum was a demented place of mind games with hearts as cold as limestone and intentions as dark as a spiritual abyss. Outwardly there were no visible fruits on this tree that drew any alarm or caused anyone to think otherwise. The branches of the asylum were like the line on a heart monitor bearing no pulse, flat and dead. Behind the scenes Dr. Rutowski drew sap from the weaken soil of his patients' minds. Their minds in the eyes of the Widow Maker had been perfectly twisted, roped, and looped together like a Gordian knot.

According to Greek legend the original knot had been tied by Kind Gordius of Phrygia, which an oracle later revealed would only be undone by the future ruler of Asia. Alexander the Great was presented with this knot. He quickly examined it, drew his sword, and cut it perfectly into two halves. Dr. Rutkowski had long sensed that nurse Lorraine's repeated questions concerning his unorthodox psychiatric techniques and motives for violation of basic psychiatric protocols had become a type of Gordian Knot for the Widow Maker to cut. She was the one anomaly amongst his staff that could potentially draw unwanted public attention to his dark affairs.

One evening after she had completed her final rounds for the day Lorraine stopped by Dr. Rutowski's office as she headed home. She intended to drop off the daily patient's behavioral report and was very surprised when she discovered his office was vacant. The bookcase on the side of his desk had been slightly pulled out from the wall. It exposed an entryway into another room. Cautiously she stepped closer. Still, she kept enough distance to remain safe. She noticed the iridescent glow of a faint light on the floor revealing a hidden staircase to an unknown lower chamber. Softly she whispered his name, "Dr. Rutowski, you in there?" No answer came. Slowly she inched closer and pulled open the bookcase just enough to get a better look inside. Suddenly a horrible scent, like that of decomposing flesh, dead rodents and bile filled her nose. She had to block off the putrid scent, so she used the long sleeve of her button-up cashmere sweatshirt to cover her nose and mouth. Disgusted she said, "My God, what is that?" Agitated, she called downstairs a second time, "Dr. Rutowski, you down there?" Her curiosity increased even more, when there was no response from him again, but she swore she heard the faint sound of movement from within the lower chamber. She had to know if he was down there. The thought also screamed inside her mind, "Why hadn't he told her about this area? More importantly, what was he doing down there at this hour?"

Lorraine activated the light on her iPhone and slowly eased through the narrow opening and descended into the Widow Maker's lair. The stench of raw sewage along with whatever else had died down there flooded her senses more and more with each step that she took. Eventually the scent became so strong that her nose burned. By the time she reached the bottom of the stairs she had an unbearable slimy taste that saturated her mouth and she vomited. Six torches lit the dark cavernous dwelling. Down there was an old cell constructed of huge parts of limestone and mud bricks, a mucky dirt floor and a secure door of rusted iron bars. There in the cell, she found a malnourished patient whom she thought had long been discharged from the Asylum. A vacant stare filled her eyes. A small incision bore a coarse thread of stitches was visible on the left side of her throat. The Widow Maker had severed her epiglottis, which controlled her tongue and vocal cords, therefore, she could not speak. She stumbled contorted to the bars in a horribly soiled patient gown. The nerves in both of her beet were completely dead from the venom of various vipers. Dr. Rutowski had recently, under the tutelage of the Widow Maker, taken up this dark practice. He induced rare strains of venom in what he called neurotic therapy to test the threshold of pain. The patient squatted in the middle of the cell and pissed a heavy stream of dark yellow ammonia nauseous urine. She slowly pulled off each of her toenails, one-by-one. She did this to relieve pressure from the sticky puss-like secretion that bubbled on her toes. The result of a venomous infection as obscene as stage four cancer and left her feet covered with multiple incurable sores. Slowly she lifted herself up from the floor. She wiped herself with the tail of her soiled gown and walked over to nurse Lorraine.

Lorraine cried out amid a panic filled terror attack,

"Oh my God! Oh my God! Don't worry, I'm going to get you out of there." Lorraine shook the door hard and tried to open it. Suddenly she became aware that the patient stood there and pointed to someone behind her. She had barely peeked over her shoulder when she saw the Widow Maker's eyes that appeared to hover in the darkness. She gasped as he quickly wrapped his massive hand around her slender throat and violently jammed three highly polished nickels into each of her eyes. Hysterically, she yelled while violently swinging to try to free herself from her attacker. Still her small stature remained like an unwanted ragdoll in his strong grip. Afterwards the six nickels were deposited into her eyes to pay a fee to the Boatman Charon.

The Widow Maker discarded his new toy momentarily and listened to her agonized cries and watched her grope blinded down the hallway. Repeatedly she screamed for help as she felt her way along the wall toward the staircase. This seemed to excite the Widow Maker even more. He mocked her in a low malicious tone from several places in the dark, "Lux Ab Exitium Velle Venere," over and over again. After a while he went silent and all that could be heard were the sounds of her cries that whimpered with short sporadic breaths. Just as she felt the wall disappear indicating that indeed she had reached the staircase, out of nowhere he appeared behind her. Her deafening scream coursed through the air as he plunged the first blade through her back and scarped the fourth vertebrae of her spine. He hooked the ridged teeth of the blade that was made from the jawbone of an ass underneath her ribcage. Its teeth firmly latched onto her breastbone. With one swift pull he lifted her feet from the pavement and dragged her off into the darkness. A thick river of blood mixed with mucus and saliva flowed like lava from her mouth.

One-by-one Lorraine's shoes came off as he dragged her down the hall toward an acid filled earthen pit. The patient in the cell smiled like an awestruck bride as she reached mindlessly through the bars and grabbed the forgotten pair of shoes. She knew she could never place them on her damaged feet. Slowly she cradled them in her arms and nestled them to her breast like a small suckling child. Then she turned and walked back into the same dark corner of her cell from which she had emerged.

At the far end of the hall the Widow Maker flung Lorraine's twitching corpse into the earthen pit. Quietly he stood there in a trance and wiped her blood from the first blade onto his white lab coat. Slowly her clothes floated while her skin expanded, bubbled, and liquefied in the shallow grave.

CHAPTER 5
STAFF OVERSITE

———◇○⊂⦆⊃○◇———

There are three basic types of people that work at every secure mental health facility across America. First, there are those who are there because they believe the work has value and that they can make a difference. Second, there are those who are there simply because of job security. They punch a clock, mind their business, and go home to tend to their families. To them, everyone at their job is either someone they must share a task with or a file number they must process. Third, are those who in just one encounter with them the mind wonders, "What in the hell are you doing working here?" They carry themselves more like they belong on the evaluation side of the clipboard rather than the monitor's side. They display extremely poor social etiquette skills. They often appear as if they are coming down off some illicit drug. A drug which their dealer just told them 'Sorry dude, but nobody sells that shit anymore.'

Undesirable environments such as Stonewall Asylum are known to breed abnormal complexities involving staff and patient relations. A majority of these interactions result in ways that subtly defy, but in other ways blatantly undermine professional expectations. One by which the norms of a therapeutic community are deemed societally acceptable, appropriate, and safe. Absence of staff consistency in a therapeutic community has the ability to plunge its decorum and civility into a nuclear winter of bitterness. Acts of insensitivity are magnified and perceived as degrading. In a flash of anger, the attitude of the person on either side of the coin can quickly go from being like sugar to being like shit. Slowly the guillotine of retribution is pulled and set in cue to sever the head of a newly acquired mortal enemy.

Out of all the shortcomings of the residential care staff at Stonewall Asylum, none had a more plagued mind with a convict mentality than one staff member named Chico Rivera. Underneath his warm angelic smile, he was a low-life and a pusher of prescription pills of all sorts. He was a false dream peddler and a psychological predator of the mentally ill. He was the epitome of a man that many believed was undeserving of God's air in his lungs. He built a steady clientele of patients who looked to forget the mental anguish surrounding the circumstances that brought them to the Asylum. Cunningly he masked his true intentions to make a profit off their pain, especially those like Cara, his favorite.

She was very attractive, but often walked about the grounds with wild mangled hair on top of her head or draped forward to hide her face. She held a dirty baby doll in her arms that was partially wrapped in swaddling cloth. The doll was a symbol of her infant child that she had martyred like Andrea Yates did her children. Chico River, like a child, constantly picked at the scab that covered her mind because it fascinated him. Deviously he lured her into a darker hole within herself. A hole filled with powerful antipsychotics, cheap vodkas, broken promises, and uncontrollable lusts. Eventually it pulled her mind back from reality like a heavy pendulum. The continual flood of extreme emotions behind repeated abuse of unregulated dosages of Zyprexa combined with extreme mental stimulation from bouts of mania, mixed fantasy, and reality along with frequent sexual stimulation caused her mind to lock. A tragic end, but that is not how it started with Cara.

It all happened so fast. It took less than two and one-half months and she was emotionally sprung. Chico secretly sent Cara letters under a female name. They were extravagant love lies about how he wanted to be with her. Every day he whispered to her excitedly, "Hey beautiful!" while she walked laps around the main hall with another girl. The other girl was very shy, way too shy to ever tell. Together the two girls giggled, but only Cara looked back in acknowledgement. Although she was very beautiful, at least three notches above the type of women he normally cheated on his wife with. There was the occasional less-attractive patient, which filtered through the court ordered psychiatric evaluation, with a body he could not resist. He had an eye for unchaste women such as this; women by which he could easily tell she was just a little sluttier than Cara.

Once Cara caught him coming out of a mop closet with another girl. Angrily she stomped off while trying to save face in front of her friend. While she patted the dingy plastic baby doll that represented her dead infant child she told her friend, "Come with me Zoey is getting cranky and tired. Maybe she is wet. I should go change her diaper."

Later on, that night, Chico Rivera went to Cara's room during the last medication and snack round. She was completely bare-chested sitting on the bed breast feeding her baby. He played on her delusion that she should forgive him because Zoey needs her father, that the other girl meant nothing to him, and he was just helping her to get some gum out of her hair. Cara gave in and let him pull into her from behind. Meanwhile, he told her she was a good mother and wife. When he was done and turned to leave, she said, "Try not to stay out too late. I may need help with the baby in the middle of the night." He smiled and said, "Sure thing honey. I'll be home soon." He had not realized it, but amid his lust driven deception he had dropped several packets of Zyprexa from his pants pockets on the bed.

Cara had taken six of the thirteen pills she found in the small manila envelopes. That night she suffered a violent seizure behind the powerful antipsychotic. When her mind finally struggled to reset it swung back with such force that it locked above her homeostasis margin (the point of normality in brain wave patterns) and permanently damaged her prefrontal lobe. This pendulum crashed against the fragile barrier of her mind like it was a thin piece of glass that once covered a jewelry box knocked from a dresser to a floor. Her conscious reasoning fractured within herself, and she never latched onto reality again.

The following morning Cara was discovered missing at breakfast. Quietly she sat catatonic in her room with her baby on the floor while snot dripped from her nose. A vacant stare filled her eyes as she slowly mumbled. Her mind was no longer able to formulate a complete thought. Dr. Rutowski was notified immediately after the envelopes were found. He immediately checked the cameras and medication logs. Dr. Rutowski began to hear the familiar chime of six nickels falling to the ground as his vision grew hazy. The Widow Maker's gaze narrowed on the security monitor as Chico Rivera stepped out of Cara's room and adjusted his belt and shirt. He froze the frame as Rivera looked up and directly into the camera. A sinister smile formed on his face. Closely he whispered into the security guard's ear,

"Summon Chico Rivera to my office at once and notify Ms. Sharai to prepare his termination papers at once." The guard replied, "Yes sir. I'll see to it at once Dr. Rutowski."

Dr. Rutowski was certain another patient knew about this relationship. He would find out who and deal with them later. For now, he moved Cara to an unmarked isolation room on a wing used primarily for dry storage. He sternly warned the two orderlies helping her from her wheelchair onto the bed, "Don't breathe a word concerning Cara's whereabouts to any of the other staff. I'd prefer to brief them myself. Especially not a word to the city officials that frequent through here or anyone for that matter outside of this facility who may ask in general how things are going over here at the Asylum. Less word of an incident of this magnitude concerning a patient at our new facility were to spread like a deadly virus. The mob of our critics would appear in the night carrying torches to amass a witch hunt against this administration like Donald Trump's presidency while calling for the doors to be shut immediately, destroying my greatest work and costing all of you your jobs. Although Cara will be noticeably missing from group for an extended period of time, be it that she is completely disassociated from her family due to her murdering her infant child, there's no need to suspect any visits or calls from them. I've examined the charades of letters from the staff member in question. They are untraceable to any actual residence. My guess is that he never mailed them here. Instead, he placed them among the incoming mail that one of you two passed out daily during breakfast." He said this to paint them as accomplices or negligently liable at last.

The short female orderly who was jaw to jaw with Cara locked her arms around her to lift her from the wheelchair. She paused mid lift and looked fearfully over Cara's shoulder into the eyes of the taller male orderly, who had placed his hand flat against Cara's back to balance her. As if he had heard the whispered prayers from their hearts say, 'I sure hope there's a way out of this.'

Dr. Rutowski continued, "It is very unfortunate that a staff member has taken advantage of someone in our care and dragged you two into this mess. However, I see no reason why we can't deal with this in house. I assure you requital will com." Upon stating that he began to hear the familiar chime of six nickels falling to the ground as his vision grew hazy. The orderlies nodded quickly in agreement and left.

The Widow Maker removed Dr. Rutowski's glasses from his face and started to clean the lenses with a damp cloth from his back pocket. He spoke low to himself as he turned into the hall, "I wonder what lies will he try to offer to evade The Boatman. Well, he wouldn't be the first to offer the Reaper a tip."

The Widow Maker stood in the hall outside the cracked door of Dr. Rutowski's office and listened for several minutes. This was so he could divine the wickedness in Chico Rivera's heart. After listening to him pace back and forth while he rehearsed his lies like people do when summoned before a judge, he pushed the door open just a tad bit as Rivera Walked away. When he turned back towards the door, he quickly noticed the piercing gaze of the Widow Maker's eyes. They rested on him as he continued to meticulously polish Dr. Rutowski's glasses. Though Chico Rivera was not aware of it, the pupils of his eyes dilated several centimeters. His voice tone spiked several decimals just before he began to stutter like many others attempting to lie. To the Widow Maker his words were like government promises constructed of half-truths and full of holes. He said, "I swear to you Dr. Rutowski, I had no idea she had taken that many pills. The Widow Maker responded, "Why that's because you were too busy sticking your hand in the cookie jar."

He never suspected the cloth in the Widow Maker's hand had been dipped in chloroform. When he awoke, he was downstairs on a gurney. Violently he shook to try to loosen the restraints on the bed. The Widow Maker approached with a small circular saw in his hand and said, "Mind if I take a look inside?" Rivera pleaded as the sound of the small cranial saw cut down into his skull. A thick dark stream of blood poured down the side of the heavy leather strap that secured his head to the gurney. The Widow Maker smiled demented at him and said, "Since only Christ can forgive sins if its amnesty you seek you've come to the wrong place.

Don't worry, I've deemed you faultless and unable to change yourself. Fortunate for you I'm considered by many to be a thaumaturge or miracle worker of sorts. Now hold still this is very delicate work. The first 10cc's of arachnid venom should adjust your pain levels substantially for this procedure."

After the injection, the Widow Maker took a serrated knife and cut deep down into Rivera's right quadricep. He peeled back and filleted the muscle tendons open like he was harvesting a deer. Next, like an excavator having found his first jewel he said, "My, my what do we have here? looks like someone has had replacement knee surgery." Using a pair of tong-like pliers he clamped down on the shiny metallic ball joint embedded under muscle sinew, nerve endings and veined flesh. Chico Rivera's eyes rolled into the back of his head as pain shot across his mind like a commuter train with no brakes. The Widow Maker tightened his grip and spoke through gritted teeth, "Don't worry if you survive this part. I'll give you some of those lovely sedatives you've been peddling in my halls."

When he plucked the ball from its socket it made a sticky hollow suction sound like an infected tooth pulled from a mouth. The Widow Maker looked at the pliers, then at him before he passed out. When he awoke his mouth had been stitched closed with rusted twine. His arms were bound, extended at his sides by short chains nailed deep within the earth. A dingy plexiglass window separated him into a corner of the room. The Widow

Maker had several industrial strength fishing hooks, hung by long chains from the ceiling like a beaded curtain. He wasted no time in lifting Chico Rivera from the gurney and violently thrusting him onto the hooks like in a slaughterhouse. Fire filled his eyes as he narrowed his gaze and studied him. Chico Rivera screamed at the top of his lungs through his sealed mouth. Hot tears ran down his face. The Widow Maker pushed him aside and walked away as he swung lightly on the chain. Mockingly he said under his breath while he climbed the stairs back to Dr. Rutowski's office, "whoever said there's no rest for the wicked. You shall be the first edition to my live art gallery."

CHAPTER 6
MISSING MEMBERS

———⇾o◠◡○◠———

The eyes are electrical lamps reflecting the innermost thoughts of the mind. At times they are in harmony with the rest of the body. A skilled actor or actress may cleverly deceive someone with a theatrical performance and lead them to believe that they are someone they are not. However, the eyes tell a different story. Truthful people bear direct stillness in their eyes when they make contact. A story reflected off the truth of the intricacies of the mind. Sometimes the story is told grudgingly against the outward performance being displayed.

These are the things Dr. Rutowski looked for as he carefully surveyed the table. A minor expression like a twitch of the eye suggested the shovel's spade was close to a buried secret. The eyes that looked up to the left before one spoke suggested that a lie was brewing. Peering down to the right said they were remorseful about a past deed. When ashamed a trans-like stare filled their eyes behind memories they would rather forget. Dr. Rutowski searched for a flicker of deception in each pair of eyes at the table. While he sat in deep conscious thought. His dark counterpart subconsciously condemned everyone in the room. Dr. Rutowski wanted to investigate the matter at hand. Meanwhile, The Widow Maker eagerly looked to place his next wager at this high stakes poker table for souls. Forcefully he made dark lead impressions with a pencil onto the notepad by Dr. Rutowski. Repeatedly he wrote backwards with his left hand next to Dr. Rutowski's glass of water, "One by land, two by sea, the Widow Maker is coming for thee."

Dr. Rutowski did a quick head count to ensure that all able-bodied residents were present and accounted for. When he was done, he reached to take a sip of water and noticed the strange acrylic like letters that read sadistic thoughts of his dark psyche. This was not something he was prepared to deal with at the time. So, he searched through is notepad for some notes from the last group session. While he turned page after page worry grew steadily in his heart. The Latin inscription, "Lux Ab Exitium Velle Venere," was scribbled mindlessly on each side of the paper. His mouth dried like sand. His stomach knotted and tensed. He knew he had opened Pandora's Box and had no way of closing it. He had unleashed the Widow Maker upon these already ravaged souls. Now he could do nothing except sit back and watch carnage unfold.

He dropped his head and let the voices of those around him fade from his mind. For the first time in a very long time the great Dr. Marcus Rutowski was lost and did not know what to do. The more he gave it thought the more the story began to unfold in his mind's eye. He began to see that the Widow Maker was a true jedi master and he his unskilled, rather predictable padawan. He saw how he had used Carlos MacIntyre as a pawn to send him the journal. That he orchestrated all the circumstances surrounding him quitting his prestigious position at the University of Minnesota and acquiring Stonewall Asylum. The whole thing was his brainchild, and he was simply along for the ride. So, if this is what he had discovered, and it was only the beginning. What was the Widow Maker's end game?

No intruder breaks into a house to merely admire another's possessions. No, they either come to take something or leave an item to later be found. He knew the Widow Maker had a purpose behind this cultured hell he had created. Did he want to live? It was his job to heal the fracture in his patient's minds and protect them, if need be, even from themselves. Now he wondered how could he help restore their minds when his was under siege by the Widow Maker? How could he possibly protect them when at the same time the opposing force of his dark side was hunting them?

Professionally he understood that on the real-world side of his patient's despairing minds many of their families were missing, which made it very difficult for them to cope with the very real circumstances surrounding their placement at the Asylum. Every trace of birthdays, holidays, social connections as well as childhood memories diminished under a debilitating illness until they were gone. Unrecognizable images like old photographs from a forgotten time with scratched faces blurred like an incantation by an apparition in their minds after some had experienced significant mental breakthroughs at the asylum. Their body language and social interaction skills dramatically changed and increased with confusion. They became plagued with retarded psychomotor activity as if they had been suddenly flushed from the matrix of their personality derangements, then forced to accept the fact that they had been fed a lie. The family they thought they had only existed in a dream world. No blue pill was strong enough to carry their mind back to the comfort of the lies it had nested in. The asylum was real, and no one was coming to save them from the monster that lurked in its halls.

There was one girl who felt lost at the asylum. Allison had an obscure personality, paucity of thought and minimal speech. She ate all her meals alone in her room. She sat quietly in isolated corners during therapy groups or just outside the circle with her face concealed by her hair. She avoided making too much eye contact and slept much of her day away. Her existence had become emotionally numb. Her mind blank behind vacant eyes that bore very little light. When agitated by a painful revisiting of memories, condemning eyes and distasteful comments from the past, she would beat the palms of her hands against her head, nervously tap an index finger on the chair and yell, "He's coming, he's coming for you, and he'll find you! There's nowhere that any of you can hide!"

The staff had grown accustomed to her dark tangents and dismissed them as nothing. Now the more Dr. Rutowski listened to her the more he wondered. Did this woman intuitively know something that he and the others had missed? Was she the one whom he was looking for?

Truth sometimes can be baffling to deal with. The threat of a virus about to prematurely extinguish or shrewdly cripple a child's life. The young teenage mind with no criminal background plus outstanding accolades in educational achievement, who unleashes a murderous plot against a local synagogue. The famed writer like John Singleton at the pinnacle of his career suddenly dies at age 51. Most baffling to Dr. Rutowski was the simple truth that there were more things that bonded him and the Widow Maker than things that divided them. Right now, was their common need to silence the innocent. Which in essence was a heinous crime in order to conceal justice. However, much he desired to protect her, protecting their legacy was far more important.

While he pondered as to what he should do about her. Suddenly he began to hear the familiar chime of six nickels falling to the ground as his vision grew hazy. The Widow Maker whispered to him, "It is apparent that you lack the stomach and the skill required in this area. Fortunately for both of us I bear no sentiment in dealing with such matters. I will deal with her myself. Prepare her discharge papers at once or shall I have Chico Rivera assist me?" His voice trailed off with a low dark chuckle.

Dr. Rutowski whispered lowly to himself, "Chico Rivera. What have I done?" He passed his reflection momentarily and looked down at the table and asked, "What's happening to me? Last, I remember I was talking with the two orderlies that helped bring the patient to the secure room off the administration wing. Then I blacked out. Next thing I recall I was sitting at my desk overlooking some files." Several staff members present in the room mumbled to themselves, "What is he talking to himself about?"

Nevaeh Sharai watched him closely but said nothing. Thick salt-like beads of sweat covered his forehead and his hands were sweating profusely. He reached for his pen that the Widow Maker had been writing with. He fumbled and accidently dropped it on the floor. Quickly he reached down to pick it up. When he did, he noticed the red clay-like dirt on the tips and soles of his shoes from the floor of the basement chamber.

Two stories below ground in the chamber sounds of chains rattling and agonizing moans from Chico Rivera were muffled at the far end of the hall. The eyes of the other captive patient peered through the darkness at the faint light at the bottom of the staircase. She motioned down the hall to Rivera until she got his attention. Then she placed a finger over her lips as if to say, "Quiet or he'll come back."

Nevaeh Sharai watched Dr. Rutowski carefully as he arose and made haste toward his office. She could tell that he was growing increasingly disturbed day by day. His level of unpredictability was without a doubt connected to the evolution of his own dark psychosis. Like a symbiotic parasite that not only feeds on its host but learns to mimic and eventually replace the original organism. She understood that the man in front of her was no longer her colleague, her mentor, and her friend. Only a faint trace remained of the man that she had once greatly admired. Her suspicion was that his dark psychosis was merely replicating routines and behaviors that it had once seen Dr. Rutowski display. What she actually had been witnessing was the clever theatrics of the Widow Maker. This was so he could hide in plain sight. If there were any tracers of that brilliant mind left, how much longer could it endure before its light was finally extinguished by eternal darkness?

Suddenly Nevaeh Sharai felt an ice-cold hand brush one of the sandy brown curls of her hair from above her right eye. Raquel said, "Pretty. You remind me of my daughter." Startled, Nevaeh said, "Now Raquel, we've talked about respecting others personal space." Raquel leaned in closer to Nevaeh, her hair was in nappy plats on her head, her breath smelled horrible, her gums and teeth sticky from infection and decay. She whispered, "You can't save him. He won't leave this place. He's nested like the others before him."

Nevaeh asked, "Who are you talking about? Save who? Leave from where? Here at the asylum?" Raquel just smiled as she stood and walked over to the spot where she normally conversed with herself at by the wall. Nevaeh watched as an orderly went over and talked to Raquel to try and get her to return to the group. Unsuccessful, the orderly returned to a small huddle of staff members that were discussing something disturbing amongst themselves.

Several minutes of muffled comments and distracted stares by staff penetrated the window. Nevaeh signaled for Sam Green to wrap up his sharing time about what led him to the Asylum. She arose and went over to Raquel who repeatedly whispered dark things in a playful child-like voice to herself. Nevaeh softly asked, "Raquel, would you like to share something with the group before we close? Everybody has had a chance to process a memory from their past with the group except you."

The chatter of staff grew louder in irritation. Distracted Nevaeh whispered to one staff whose eyes she caught, "If you need to discuss something please take it in the hall while we're in group." When she refocused her attention on the wall, Raquel was repeatedly whispering with a tempo that increased each cycle. She counted aloud while touching thumb to al her fingertips on one hand. "One, two, three, four, five, six," over and over again. Nevaeh watched as she slowly raised her other hand and pointed outside the window. When she looked outside, she saw Dr. Rutowski pacing back and forth on the front lawn in the cold sleet rain. He had no umbrella. His beige jacket was open, his clothing was as wet as the notepad under his arm. He repeatedly tapped a pencil six times against the side of his temple. Nevaeh quickly closed the blinds and whispered to staff to stop the group and temporarily return all the patients to their rooms. Then she quickly grabbed two blankets from the hall and headed outside to get Dr. Rutowski.

CHAPTER 7
VISUAL TRICKERY

Tthere are roughly 1 in 25 Americans that suffer from a severe form of mental illness. There are over 3 million African Americans in this country that have a form of mental illness. That is enough people to populate the city of Los Angeles twice over. The combined number of undiagnosed US cases who currently suffer from a form of mental illness is estimated to reach well into the tens of millions. Most of these troubled individuals have no one to turn to. They exist in our communities under the stereotypes of being hardheaded, misunderstood, troublemakers, wild and in some cases just damn fools. Since mental illness can be hereditary some people label entire families with these negatives stigmatizes.

However, mental illness is not always the result of a

natural biological disorder. Sometimes it is the nurtured result of a social environment embedded with distorted ideologies. Often in mainstream American society it is chemically cultivated behind years or sometimes a single episode of mind-altering drug use. It appears that somewhere along the way someone forgot to tell us. Altering brain chemistry or as some call it, getting high, is actually playing mad scientist with one's own mind. Mentally ill is not just a classification for those that register under a licensed psychiatrist, suffer from schizophrenic hearing or visual delusions, and are prescribed various 13 syllable unpronounceable forms of medications. Truth of the matter is those who are on prescribed meds often have a better grasp on reality than those who are not. Mental illness in clarity is a psychological deprivation of reasoning. Characterized by an inability to function long term within the norms of society and manage the basic routines of one's own life.

It devastated Nevaeh Sharai to see Dr. Rutowski in his current mental state. She sighed out of despair. Lately she had begun to long for her former cozy little reception area. Things were so different on the University of Minnesota campus in downtown Minneapolis. The environment was socially energized. The clients had some level of societal functionalism that they ascribed to. Dr. Rutowski was well organized in his private caseload.

Dr. Rutowski was till an active and highly respected

part of the university's faculty. He taught, lectured, and challenged every student he encountered to think outside of the box. Dare to be original and not simply go along with the status quo. Then one day he received an unexpected phone call from a former student. She told him that she was gravely concerned about her son and had no one else to turn to. Not many days after that he met Carlos MacIntyre for the first time. Everything he thought he knew about psychiatry changed. It seemed to her that overnight he became a recluse. He grew obsessed with reading a journal that came anonymously by mail courier one snowy day. He soon began to reschedule his clients. His repeated absence from several classes of which he had personally designed and taught for years alarmed the university to conclude that he was either overworked or under a tremendous amount of stress. Consequently, his classes were reassigned. Suddenly Nevaeh laughed at her own delusion. She thought about how she responded to the sudden news of moving the practice to break new ground. This ground was an isolated compound completely cut off from the rest of the world.

Dr. Rutowski had become completely unable to manage his own mental health, let alone fulfill his role as head of psychiatry at Stonewall Asylum. Despite all his hurtful comments and threats to have her visa revoked, she remained loyal and told herself that the Dr. Marcus Rutowski she knew would have never addressed her with such degradation. Nonetheless, he had developed an iciness about his decorum. His dark side had virtually engulfed his attitude.

Vain is the net that is set in the sight of any bird. Methodically this Egyptian Blackness appeared to wield a twisted desire to net the unintelligible mind. A mind ripe for cruelty and inhumane punishment whose sins cry to be recompensed. This caused Nevaeh to contemplate the plight of the patients. She had witnessed firsthand many of the shrewd and unmerciful acts of the Widow Maker. That he seemed to savor each moment while he mentally tortured several patients. One patience at St. Peter's Psychiatric Hospital was so terrified she defecated on herself.

Many images of old Henry Lee Stonewall flashed fresh through her mind. After all it was her who found his severed head in the woodshed. Three nickels slotted each of his missing eyes. Slivers from the leather arm pad on his wheelchair were under his fingernails. An indicator that at the time of his murder he clawed the armrest in search of his help bell. It had been crushed again on the edge of the handle by some sort of a steel pipe. Although he was loathed by many, she was certain someone from the grounds had killed him, but by whom? The first answer came to her mind of Dr. Rutowski, she quickly shrugged off.

She had spent far too much time distracted by the administrative and external operations of the asylum. Meanwhile, someone was picking off the patients. Plus, two staff members had quit or, so she had been told. Was this true or did something else happen to them? What if there was a patient who knew their timed rotations and perfectly planned each malicious act? Then sat cleverly masked with an impudent face. She had to speak to Dr. Rutowski about these matters for all their safety was in dire straits.

Later, that night she made sure that all the patients were secure in their rooms. Then she stopped to check on Dr. Rutowski before retiring for the night. When she arrived at his private quarters he was not there. His bed looked as if he had not slept in it for days. She found a patient's file she thought had long been discharged on the nightstand under the window.

A storm slowly rumbled outside. Lightning flashed as Nevaeh bent to pick up the file. When she looked up Dr. Rutowski's reflection was in the window from the hall behind her. When she noticed his reflection from the cast of the storm's lightning she quickly straightened up, turned, and cuffed the file behind her back and said, "I was doing round and thought I felt a draft on this wing. Naturally, I double checked all the windows for security." He glanced at the digital thermostat and said, "It's 71 degrees in here, which is warmer than I like. Maybe you're coming down with something due to the change in weather?" Nevaeh smiled politely and said, "God I hope not. Maybe I should make a nice cup of chamomile tea to warm up. Would you like a cup?" With a look of concern he said, "No, no I'm fine. You enjoy your tea and get some rest. General staff can manage for the night." He paused momentarily and looked down at the floor. His thoughts drifted toward the basement chamber. He continued, "I have a few things that require my immediate attention. Best I take a raincheck on that chamomile tea. Perhaps tomorrow afternoon we can catch up?"

He quickly turned and pulled a journal from the small drawer of the other nightstand by the bed. He tucked it tightly under his arm, turned toward the hall and briskly headed out of the room. Nevaeh eyed him curiously with his coveted possession. Then it dawned on her, that journal was the same one a mail courier had delivered to the Minneapolis office after Carlos MacIntyre went missing. Immediately, Dr. Rutowski became fascinated, even obsessed with its savage entries. The next morning when she arrived at work, Nevaeh sat her things down and went to make tea, but the mahogany serving platter was still gone. She proceeded to pull the files she needed for the morning sessions to drop them off at his office. When she opened the door, she could instantly tell that he had been there all night. The chamomile tea she had set for him the previous night was still untouched. He stared at the floor as he paced back and forth from the sliding glass patio door to his desk. His arms were folded tightly across his chest. He repeatedly tapped a pencil against his left temple six times while he contemplated the five Latin words that he kept mumbling. She suddenly realized that that was the moment everything changed in him. A year later the moral decline of his attitude, behavior and speech astonished her. She thought to herself that there had to be some kind of connection between everything that was happening to him now and that journal. She had to get her hands on it.

Nevaeh ran into the hall and called after Dr. Rutowski, "Well, I did want to speak with you about roles and responsibilities with the current caseload. There will be many questions regarding several incidents over the last few weeks." She measured her next words very carefully and hoped he still had the capacity to fully grasp what was at stake. She continued, "There will be a significant need for either you or myself to tend to growing matters outside of group, while the other focuses more on needs of clients." She smiled passively, gave a polite nod and concluded, "As your assistant I normally tend to the bulk of administrative paperwork behind the scenes. Now given my familiarity with your behavioral management techniques, if you're willing, I'd like to spend a little more time with the caseload sir. Since it's typically a small group to monitor. I feel overwhelmed with management of these vast grounds. Plus, construction costs are way over budget, and I don't know why."

Dr. Rutowski spoke up over his shoulder as he hurried down the hall, "Let's revisit this tomorrow about noon Nevaeh." Her steps picked up in stride behind him as she further petitioned, "But Dr. Rutowski, what about morning affairs?" When he tried to respond he began to hear the familiar chime of six nickels falling to the ground as his vision grew hazy.

The piercing gaze of the Widow Maker turned and rested on her. Nevaeh instantly became afraid. The soft visage before her had changed. Now a soul drinking stare swept over her flesh. She quickly stopped. The Widow Maker smiled and beckoned her closer as he said, "Why Ms. Sharai, you look like a mouse trapped inside a Skinner's Box with no achievable exit except the window behind you. Ah, and I see you still have that lovely piece of cheese behind your back." Nevaeh said nothing and slowly took one step back. When she did the Widow Maker slowly took one step toward her. One step, two steps, three steps, each time she took a step he matched hers. Once closer, her eyes darted to the side at the open room door and then back on him. When his smile widened showing the pearl white molars in his mouth. Her eyes widened in fear as he leaned forward like an Olympic sprinter. Navaeh quickly turned and darted into the room and slammed the door.

She had barely moved the dresser to block the door when the Widow Maker charged and hit the door with the full weight of his body. He slid the dresser six to eight inches from the door. Nevaeh screamed as she tried to hurry and push the dresser back. Deranged eyes filled the cracked doorway as he said, "Now stop this erratic behavior and unbarricade this door. I know, we could have some of that chamomile tea you like so much and discuss this urgent matter that can't wait until tomorrow." Nevaeh yelled, "No, no, don't worry about it. It can wait until tomorrow." Instantly the Widow Maker stopped pushing. The door slammed shut as she pushed with all her strength. She wedged herself on the floor with her feet braced against the bed and her back against the dresser.

The pupils of the Widow Maker's eyes split and revealed a smaller set in each outer corner. They dilated wide like the Mad Hatter while he taunted her, "Teatime, teatime, teatime," over and over again. Hot tears ran down her face as she held her breath in fear. Softly she whimpered child-like, "Please go away. I don't want any tea." After several minutes he stopped. Her heart rate slowed as she wiped her eyes and nose with the sleeve of her blouse. She wondered if he had left. Suddenly a cruel sadistic voice whispered mockingly to her, "Are you positive you don't want to talk with me over tea my child?" Nevaeh cried, "Dr. Rutowski, help me." The Widow Maker struck the door with all his force, cracked one of the panel boards and walked off. Nevaeh sat there and cried until she fell asleep, wedged between the bed and the dresser on the floor.

Part 2: Washing of The Mind

Chapter 8
Genesis of Thought

<hr/>

There are a growing number of prominent figures in the cognitive based therapy field that share in a common belief. The belief is that the only effective way to accurately diagnose a personality derangement is to first locate the source of volatility. The god particle of the cosmos. Be it the intentional devious acts of another person or the careless self-inflicted experimental trauma. That in the end strapped the mind to a booster rocket of abstract reality, created a Goldilocks system of habitable planets and landed on the barren surface of mental abomination. This is known as the "Arson Approach". For it is the same way a fire chief would determine the actual cause of a fire. Only once careful analysis has determined the accelerant that burned down the mind. May the root cause be treated, and cognitive recalibration become successful. Cognitive disorders follow the same patterns as viscous weeds. They have deep roots. No matter how much you treat the surface with water, sunlight, vitamin, and even fresh soil. Unless you dig deep and remove the root, they will grow back over time and choke the life out of everything around it.

Although at times it appeared Dr. Rutowski had won the good fight against the dark mind of the Widow Maker, there were still slivers of the dark mind that eclipsed his sun of thought like a barren moon over the forest of uncertain days ahead. Nevaeh Sharai knew that when dealing with a drowning victim if not careful she could be pulled under too. As the days moved on, she positioned herself like a triage nurse on the battlefield of his mind. Not just for his good, but also for the good of those who would suffer in the wake thereof under his care. She understood there had been casualties. The cold reality that stole her thoughts daily caused a little bit of her soul to die nightly and made her scream at the heavens, "Why God, why?" The fact that no matter what she did to stop the carnage that steadily unfolded before her eyes, the main person she wanted to save she could not save at all.

She had discovered that true death was not an abstract reality, but an actual being. He had come for them and stood shrouded in thick darkness amongst a field of black coffins. It was then that she realized her only rational objective, "Save as many as possible" before the final battle of Armageddon begins. Over the next few weeks, a subtle fear settled down on the impatient group. No matter what the day's topic was, when it was Raquel's turn to speak, she quickly changed the subject to the hallway. In a low, dry, whisper, with wide eyes underneath spotted disheveled hair and ring wormed scalp she said, "I heard it again last night in the halls." Emily asked, "What did you hear?" Sam Green, who barricaded himself in his room nightly said, "It was nothing. Now can we please move on? I have something to share."

Nevaeh watched him closely. She had never heard Sam offer to share. She also knew that he wanted to avoid Emily's remarks. Emily smiled deviously. She relished the frightful look in the eyes of the other patients. Then, as if she could see them afraid in their rooms at night, she stuttered in a scared theatrical voice, "O-o-oh, I hope it wasn't bats. I heard something outside my window too." She said this to manipulate Raquel into terrifying the other patients. She hated it when no one believed the things she claimed she saw. With coherent eyes that were as clear as a winter's night sky, she began to describe many peculiar things she had seen at night. Nevaeh listened while Raquel described the sound of hard soled dress shoes at the end of the hall. A muffled scream that came through the floor. A dark towering figure standing outside her door. The echo of some strange Latin words in the hall. Room doors opening, patients being taken in the middle of the night. Then coins falling to the floor.

Terrified, every patient slept with their room doors locked except for one, Emily. The Widow Maker looked past collecting her several times. He saw her soul as a blight against nature even more dark than his own. She liked to sit up at night and role play conversations in her mind. Ones where everyone did what she wanted without question and only said things that agreed with her. Anyone who had challenged her throughout the day became her mortal enemy at night. There was one incident where she tried to set a girl on fire. She sneaked into her room while she was still asleep and cut the cord on her small personal fan with a pair of fingernail clippers. Then she plugged it in and tucked the cord under the girl's blanket. A staff member doing rounds noticed her leave the room and thought it was suspicious. When questioned, Emily lied and said she was only closing the room door because it was noisy, and she wanted her to get a good night's sleep.

The staff member, knowing Emily's history, quickly reopened the door and saw the cord going under the blanket, but the fan was still on the table. The patient awoke when the staff snatched the blanket back. Luckily for her the thick cover was designed for heat. This was one of the many other wicked things Emily did. So, the staff eventually labeled her the Down Syndrome Killer.

The repeated reports of nighttime disturbances caused most of the psychiatric support staff to seek employment elsewhere. Additional treatment services were cancelled altogether and several of the grounds staff members were let go. With only a skeleton crew working primarily during the daytime the level of sanitation and personal care quickly diminished at the asylum. The facility looked as if it had been overrun in a zombie apocalypse. The trash cans seemed to overflow. Most of the rooms were poorly lit or completely closed for use. The blinds and curtains on the windows remained pulled tightly. Internal security measures became quite lax. Instead of a double guard round every thirty minutes, one guard did a quick headcount every three hours or so. With only two kitchen staff members present in the afternoon the facility soon provided only one hot meal per day at dinner. Breakfast consisted of a plastic bag of dry cereal, a piece of fruit and milk. Lunch was an assortment of military rations.

While time moved on and with it the conscience of everyone that still worked at the asylum. The divide in Dr. Rutowski's mind grow. He often paced back and forth in front of the live gallery that the Widow Maker had built in the basement chamber. Adamantly they argued while he tried to sway the dark mind of Requital from bestowing another hellish fate upon one of their captives. No matter how much he tried to reason with this Egyptian Blackness, that they had gotten sloppy, and that things were way out of hand. The Dark One seethed even more that his work was not done.

Dr. Rutowski wrapped his arms around his waist. He shook himself in a deranged, twisted motion and snatched off his glasses each time the Widow Maker seized the light to speak. When he recovered the light, he calmly set his glasses back on his face and pushed them back up the bridge of his nose. Meanwhile, his facial expression shifted from passive, timid, and unsure to aggressive, firm, and calculated. Even his voice changed from low with a slight crackle to loud and highly agitated. Those bound downstairs in the chamber wondered what in the hell was happening to him, and what did this mean for their fate?

Dr. Rutowski stuttered while he pushed his glasses up the bridge of his nose, "You can't continue on this path. These are innocent, very sick individuals we're dealing with here." The Widow Maker stopped and snatched the glasses from his face then snapped back, "There are three things that are NEVER satisfied, yea, four things say not, it is enough; the grave, and the barren womb, the earth that is not filled with water, and the fire that saith not, it is enough. If there be a fifth it is me, the Widow Maker." Dr. Rutowski removed a handkerchief from his back pocket. Briskly, he started to pace again while he cleaned the lens of his glasses. Meanwhile, he pleaded all the more with the ne plus ultra of Animus, "I don't see how much more that guard you've tortured for days now can endure. I move that we should turn him over to the authorities promptly." Quickly he placed his glasses back on his face as advocated, "He must be judged by a jury of his peers." His body contorted as the Widow Maker ripped open the white blood-spattered lab coat that they wore. He snatched the glasses from his face and said, "Here in this asylum I am judge, jury, and executioner. I have only begun to tear his sentence from his flesh and carve my name upon his soul." Those who stood by in the chamber were mortified by those words. They understood clearly that their captor was extremely demented after they had witnessed how he had ranted and raved back and forth with himself against himself.

These two distinct souls were engaged in a power struggle over one body. The more they argued the more the mind of Dr. Rutowski waned like the flicker of a flame against the boisterous wind. The psyche of the Widow Maker overpowered and evolved rapidly, existentially. His dark will soon encapsulated the good doctor and fully permeated his being. He had normally appeared in Albert Einstein-like attire. He wore plain linen trousers, clean white dress shirts, suspenders, and soft leather crock-like shoes. Now, that image was like a mirage in the minds of his captives. Now, he stood regularly in dark torturous therapy sessions behind the closed doors of his office. While he wore a blood-spattered white lab coat. The signature garment of the Widow Maker. Various highly venomous, poisonous vipers, scorpions, black mambas and rattlesnakes filled a heavy old glass tank. Those he extracted small doses of venom from. Then he skillfully used the venom to induce malaria-like fevers on selected patients to dull the pain receptors in their bodies while he filleted and fed them one to another in a cruel sadistic family-dinner-like setting.

Various wild pets littered the basement chamber in cages. Wolves, ten-pound rats, and his favorite, a murky fish tank with piranhas that bore two-inch long teeth. All of which he used to psychologically tame and temper his environment. He also created his own sadistic opera music of which he called conceptual blending. This music combined the hellish screams of the tortured with dark symphonic piano combinations from Beethoven. After several recordings throughout the night, he silenced the screams of his chosen patients by using a coarse twine to stitch their mouths closed. Then he laminated the thread line with hot wax to make it appear as if they had been born silent, unable to speak from birth.

During the day, the basement chamber was primarily quiet. Several obligations demanded Dr. Rutowski's attention throughout the grounds. Meanwhile, downstairs whispers shuffled back and forth through the dark. Some stood while others crouched in the corners of their small box-like cells. Each of them being too weak to break through the plywood walls that separated them from the person next to them. A pair of eyes wide with fear appeared to float at the back of a pitch-black cell. Meanwhile, a raspy dry voice from within the cell whispered strange and dark things. Playful and child-like she whispered as she hopped up and down, "One, two, three, four, five, six... One, two, three, four, five, six." Then she laughed like a witch in preparation to torture any that challenged her. Two of the other captives in live gallery compartments mocked the voice as being superstitiously deranged, drunken nonsense and quite mad.

Chico Rivera yelled alongside one patient, "Shut the hell up!"

There was one gorgeous Latina patient named Tina that had been in the chamber since her arrival to the asylum. Originally, she was referred there by her family attorney for therapy services. She had hoped to regain custody of her seven kids in child protection. When she arrived at his office high, Dr. Rutowski used a chloroform dipped cloth to render her unconscious. He then marked her a no show and moved her to the chamber because the Widow Maker deemed her unfit. She had been there ever since. She sobbed as she patted the thick scab over her left eye. During her last session, the Widow Maker had taken a blowtorch and held it at pencil cap's distance from her face. She screamed as the blue flame slightly brushed her skin, liquefied her eyeball, and seared the lid shut. She prayed someone would come and find her soon. While her desperation grew quietly within her. She vomited from the smell of her own feces.

CHAPTER 9
DARK SPIDER

———⊸∘⟳⟲∘⊶———

While Dr. Rutkowski gave a dark lecture to six of the nine remaining patients at the asylum. One patient was out ill, another one in physical therapy, and the last one in isolation for disruptive behavior. Nevaeh Sharai stood quietly in the corner of the small study next to a bookshelf and listened. All the patients knew the real reason Raquel was now three days in the quiet room. She had spoken strongly against Dr. Rutowski in group and committed the cardinal sin by telling a local interviewing college student about the real asylum. While Dr. Rutowski stood in front of the small group, Nevaeh fingered through fresh pages of horrors in her mind like topical index cards in a drawer at a library. She recalled the look upon the faces of a misfit group of touring students as they entered the maze of the asylum. They did not belong there, but he had chosen them all.

Dry dead leaves blew in from outside as the group stumbled through the two heavy front doors into the empty lobby. She arose from her desk to intercept, but a hand on her shoulder from Dr. Rutowski made her sit. Each of them had a black envelope in their hand formally sealed with a red piece of wax that bore the initials TWM, the invitation of the Widow Maker into the belly of the beast. Everyone turned and looked behind them when the sound of the heavy doors echoed as they closed and locked them all inside. One frightened girl jumped and dropped her pad of paper for notes and folder in her arms. Suddenly, a warm, hospitable, eloquent and relaxing voice spoke, "Good morning. I am Dr. Marcus Rutowski. Welcome to Stonewall Asylum. If my memory serves me correctly, you are Karen," he said as he pointed to the tall slender, dorky-looking blonde whose skin was as pale as the backside of an Irish man's kneecaps. She nodded in agreement. He smiled and said, "Excellent." Then he turned his gaze on yet another student. "Alexander?" he asked while nodding to a chubby looking lad who dabbed at a jelly donut stain on his sleeveless sweatshirt just below his bowtie. He in return nodded while he said, "Doctor."

"You are the easiest selection to remember Calvin," Dr. Rutowski said to the only black guy in the group who fumbled through an old satchel. He spoke very rapidly, "Thank you very much for this opportunity, Dr. Rutowski. I took the liberty of bringing you a copy of my resume. Might I add your last lecture on dual diagnostic therapy was brilliant. Especially the part about," Dr. Rutowski raised a hand and said, "Please Calvin, later. There will be plenty of time to discuss the myriad of lectures I've given over the years."

A student in the group mumbled under her breath, though her words still carried volume in the empty hall, "Brown nose." Dr. Rutowski quickly said, "That would make you Camille." He said to the anorexic white girl in Gothic style clothing. Her outfit consisted of black turtleneck skintight T-shirt, heavy blue jean jacket, dark blue skirt, and combat boots with spiked wristbands. She had on thick black eyeliner and dark purple lipstick with short choppy hair. All she said in response was, "Bingo," while she turned her head, rolled her eyes, and popped her chewing gum. Dr. Rutowski commented, "Interesting, very interesting." He turned his gaze yet again to Terrance, a transgender student undergoing hormone injections as part of his final preparation to change fully into a woman from being a man. Before Dr. Rutowski could speak, a peppered voice said, "Everyone knows me, I'm Terri." However, the smile quickly left behind Dr. Rutowski's gender opinionated response of, "Welcome Terrance." He nodded to the last individual and said, "It's a pleasure to see you again Ethan." Ethan was a four feet nine-inch-tall sophomore and recent intern there, who looked as though he had been born and bred in a lab. Slowly turning to leave he said, "All of you please follow me." A bitter demanding response firmly spoke up from the back of the group, "It's Teri!"

Dr. Rutowski began to hear the familiar chime of six nickels falling to the ground as his vision grew hazy. A soul drinking stare underscored by an angelic smile turned and fell upon Teri as the Widow Maker said, "Really. We'll have to work on that now, won't we?" Teri looked at the floor. Calvin the eager one interjected, "Some of us are very excited about rumors of a new internship program starting here at the asylum. That is said to replace several staff positions." The Dark One responded, "All of you are on my list." Like lost children they ventured further inside the lair like Hansel and Gretel by the Witch's candy to the oven. Not knowing that there was no way that the Widow Maker would ever allow either of them to leave the asylum.

The further they ventured down the hall of this elaborate maze, the more several of the students noticed the skeleton crew of staff members that abode at the asylum. When they entered the main group room Raquel rushed over to Ethan and grabbed his hand. Her eyes wide with eagerness. Her hands clammy and cold. She began to tell him about the strange occurrences that as of late had become the new norm there. Ethan almost vomited at the smell of Raquel's breath and was terrified to death by her presence. Dr. Rutowski studied him carefully, curiously while Raquel gestured frantically to him with her hands.

After several moments he sought to swiftly end this encounter. Wisely, he motioned to the group, "For those of you who are truly invested in psychiatric care beyond the mere interactions of some of our more challenged individuals there are some basic protocols that we must always follow. This is for our own safety as well as the safety of the patients in our care. Patients who may periodically feel hostile when someone invades their personal space. Why in the serialized work of a sociopath like Raquel. She could easily slit your throat with a sharp chicken bone if you got too close and you'd never see it coming, right Ethan?" Ethan quickly stepped away from Raquel and said, "Correct Dr. Rutowski, four feet at all times." The other patients watched and huddled away from the tour group as if they were all carriers of some infectious airborne disease.

Most people believe that hindsight is 20/20 vision, that when most look back, they can clearly see the moves of a chess game play out up till the inevitable checkmate. Their eyes narrow at the bait to trap. The most coveted power piece on the board, the queen. Once the queen is taken by the allure of the pawn, most opponents defense collapse. The most prolific problem that Nevaeh saw when her mind drifted back to the game between her and Dr. Rutowski was her own passivity. She had stood idly by and did nothing to defend anyone from the psychosis of the Widow Maker. Her mind cringed as her extraordinary ability to recall highly vivid details kicked in. A collage of agonized patient faces lost in a world of mental cruelty swirled before her mind's eye. Patients that in her denial of the true mental state of Dr. Rutowski she had sent to their deathbeds. Her heart pounded terribly as she recalled how just a few nights ago she was almost one of those patients.

"This is ridiculous," Nevaeh said to herself as she walked over to the window, "What would any sane person do under these circumstances? Run! No one would blame my decision in the face of self-preservation. Yes, I should leave immediately, or perhaps in the middle of the night while most of the patients are asleep. I could leave around the time when Dr. Rutowski disappears after heading to his office. That would give me a good head start, but how will I get the main gate open?" As a security precaution the gate could only be electronically opened by two separate keypads operated at the same time. One keypad was in the front lobby at the security guard's desk. The other keypad was in the guard booth next to the main gate. A booth that since the decline in staff members Dr. Rutowski always kept the keys to on his person. If somehow, she was able to get the keys or override the system with an unanswered emergency response call, who would operate the inside keypad? This meant be willing to sacrifice themselves and stay behind so that the others could escape and survive? Speaking of surviving, there were only six patients that she actually knew where they were. The six that were right in front of her. Dr. Rutowski claimed that he had discharged the other patients long ago. She had believed this too, until she found that patient's file in his room. A file she was certain that something in him wanted to kill her for. Why were the contents of that file so important? Was he trying to hide the fact that she had never left the asylum? What if none of them had left? What if they were still there or worse? There was something about the gleam in Dr. Rutowski's eyes as he spoke to her. His look told her that there were more survivors, but where? Where did he constantly disappear to? At times it was as if he vanished into thin air or simply walked through the walls. Then a horrifying thought crossed her mind. Could he be connected to the screams that permeated through the floors at night? Screams that were like the early morning dew upon the grass. Slowly it appeared and covered everything. Thick screams that saturated the soil of their minds and plowed the fields of fear in their hearts.

Nevaeh knew that the terror in the eyes of the patients at the asylum was due to the dark side of Dr. Rutowski. The warning bells going off in her mind were drowned out as Dr. Rutowski's muffled voice returned to her ears. His words were like the Dark Spider that spins a web ten times stronger than Kevlar and can easily bind human prey. At times when he spoke, he used dual hidden phrases to someone about them. They initially perceived it was about someone else. Later he repeated the phrase so they would finally make the connection.

Most disturbingly he told the group one day, "The secret to an exceptional rose is not the six to eight hours of sunlight and a wide place to spread its roots as some think. No, its cradle and fragility of life is found in warm blood and quiet darkness. The rose craves what is in the human veins. All the nitrates it desires is in that red gold. . . flowing within your arms. The rose of life craves such therapy." As well such language reminded her daily that she was trapped.

She watched as the Widow Maker performed many cruel torturous acts with fiery vengeance upon those that came across his path by false pretenses so that they could evade the judgement of mankind. She recalled how he plotted and abducted Calvin. Halfway through the tour he lured him to his office to allegedly discuss hiring him. Nevaeh thought it was very strange when he came back alone. Moments later when Karen asked where he was at, the Widow Maker told her that, "although Calvin had interned here before he regretted that he had an appointment that was necessary for him to attend. Still, he apologized for not completing the tour when I asked him to participate in it purely for moral support."

Meanwhile, Calvin sat bound in the basement chamber for moral judgement. The accusation against him was his attempt to start a rebellion and lead a coop to oust the good doctor from his authority. He had been sedated with an injection of hydrochlorothiazide in Dr. Rutowski's office. A shot that can reduce the heart rate so low a person will appear to have flat-lined. There was a small rubber meditation ball in his mouth, secured tightly by a long strip of gray duct tape wrapped about his head. He sat slumped over, unconscious in what the Widow Maker came to call the judgement seat. A medieval sitting post that looked like a cross between a baby's highchair and an old 1920s electric chair. It was made of a dark lime slick faggot wood. It had thick leather wrist straps on the arm posts of the chair. A small bell attached to a long hemp rope string rested on the earthen floor next to one of the front legs of the chair. By the other front leg was an old glass jar filled with what looked like huge leeches swimming in dirty sewage water. The Widow Maker tilted his chair backwards and water-boarded him with the dirty sewage-like water. He intentionally used a cloth with small holes in it so that the leeches could slither through. As he forcefully ingested the leeches they latched onto his trachea, esophagus, and diaphragm. Slowly they ate away at his internal tissue until he rapidly vomited through is nose and mouth while he defecated on himself.

CHAPTER 10
PUPILS OF LIES

The more Nevaeh looked back through the mirror of her past actions the more she loathed and despised herself. For the past fourteen months she had willfully gave into the darkness and submitted to the worst kinds of deceptions. Deceptions that had cost numerous lives and reinforced one dark identity. Although she never literally participated in any physical heinous act, her conscience was defiled like a glass of spring water with several drops of pig blood in it. No matter what she added to the glass to try and rationalize drinking it, still in the end she could not stomach the act. Mentally she had shown the same level of care and compassion as Andrea Yates, who gave into the worst parts of herself and brutally slayed each of her own children. Then laid them out like martyrs under a psychotic hand.

She finally accepted the fact that she was no longer Dr. Rutowski's assistant. Her colleague, mentor, and friend was gone. Whoever, whatever this was that had embodied him had a totally different agenda, one that she needed to stop by any means necessary. She could no longer be a pupil of his lies, a mere decoy or just another mental pawn on his chessboard of dark therapy. Diverting attention away from his true agenda of mass extermination and being justified in condemnation of every kind of mind puzzle he could not solve. The punishment of many extreme personality derangements turned into a candlelight vigil for their souls hosted by The Light of Death Himself. Cruel fate and dark reality steadily unfolded before her eyes like a slow-moving fog with zero visibility. Then it engulfed both the mentally strong and docile like an apex predator does its prey. This caused her to think about the deadly consequences of being caught in opposition to Dr. Rutowski. The idiopathic behavior of his dark side grew to be more twisted and demented day by day. The rapacious bloodthirsty appetite of the Widow Maker became a mad stumbling journey that tore at his mind.

Nevaeh took a deep breath and shifted her thoughts to another problem at hand. Out of the staff members that remained they all seemed completely loyal to Dr. Rutowski. Loyal enough to expose her in the blink of an eye. So, who was going to help her when the time came for her to flee and to help as many patients escape as she could? Her gaze suddenly fell upon Emily Frost. She was loyal to no one but herself. Plus, she seemed just as clever or devious as Dr. Rutowski. Nevaeh would certainly rather deal with her than with the other monster in this room. She thought about the old Persian saying, "The enemy of my enemy is my friend." Then she remembered why this was probably a bad idea. The prince who said it was betrayed by his own people.

While she thought about a temporary alliance. Emily looked her way with devilish eyes behind an impudent face and smiled. Nevaeh mumbled to herself, 'The Down Syndrome Killer, boy you sure do know how to pick'em don't you.' Emily slowly turned her gaze back to Karen in the tour group. She had a knack for spotting gullible humanitarians a mile away. Karen was shy and extremely passive. Emily could tell she had a nasty drug habit by the small needle scab marks tracked across her arms. Several of them covered a bruise from a collapsed vein in her left arm. The more she watched her the more she was reminded of her mother. Soon her curiosity peaked about the other clear imperfections that stood out about the rest of the group. Imperfections that said this entire group of students were all broken, flawed abortions unwanted by their birth families and society. That they were all under the sway of darkness, the darkness she knew lived there on the grounds of the asylum. This fascinated her to her very core.

Still there was a peculiar, unique level of mental alertness that was present in Karen unlike the other students. Many who both saw and knew her background considered her born under a terrible curse into a godless family obsessed with witchcraft and hoodoo. They saw her as someone who will roam the badlands under the shadows of condemnation, and never have the light of redemption set her free. Karen's level of awareness in the knowledge of sensations, mental operations and what passes in one's mind. Became her most powerful skill and asset to survive. Twice had her family's shack been burned down. Often, they were demonized as being a bunch of ignorant freaks. Her life stayed under constant threat at school. Eventually she dropped out and chose to take the GED test of which she barely passed. She applied for the internship at the asylum to help people with whom she felt she identified with most. Lives filled with drug use and promiscuity to numb the pain of existing. Somehow through it all, she maintained hope of leaving the bayous one day.

Nevaeh could not help noticing that there was a twisted serene look on the face of Emily. A look that said she was quite comfortable in her surroundings and desired to be no where else. By the look in the eyes of the other five remaining patients each of them had reached their breaking point. Tiny vapors of fear, anxiety, depression, insomnia, and despair arose like smoke from their flesh with a stench strong enough to arouse any subtle predator. This stirred the Widow Maker all the more. He inhaled the scent of fear as if it were a rare wine. Karen instantly noticed the shift in Dr. Rutowski's voice from his usual focused, direct, technical tone, like someone giving a book report. Then his voice became taunting, wrathfully naked backed by a mind and skill in telling a story like Dr. Hannibal Lector. He pointed out every gruesome detail about life in a way that did not appear to be human at all. He told them, "Contemplate life if you dare. The first day of life is much like the last, you come and go alone. Light shines through the doorway of darkness and who truly understands it? Of all the possible thresholds to cross you've been chosen for this one. Death the ambassador of a dying world awaits as a willing escort to guide. Will is an illusion of the mind within the grand design of true life. Come drink from the cup of destruction it beckons all flesh."

Nevaeh loved to discover coded messages from mysteries hidden inside riddles, enigmas, and secrets. Things which she personally believed was buried in all of our minds revealed within the phrases spoken from deep within the id unknowingly at times. Quickly she began to unravel the odd phrase like a cipher or cryptogram and quickly learned something very interesting. When she extracted the first word of each sentence and combined them, the phrase, "The Light of Death Will Come," appeared. She instantly recalled it was the translation of the Latin inscription, "Lux Ab Exitium Velle Venere," that Dr. Rutowski's dark side quoted often as a warning. A warning that in times past she had failed to take heed to. Suddenly she felt like

Pinocchio finally seeing his strings. The curtain had been pulled back momentarily and she saw the true face of darkness before her. Darkness made incarnate in flesh.

Quickly she left the room to go make preparations to leave. When she turned into the hallway she looked back momentarily. When she did her and Dr. Rutowski's eyes met for a brief moment and the Widow Maker waved at her with his pinky as if he knew what she was thinking. This caused Nevaeh to proceed faster down the hall. She had only a couple of minutes to pack a few things and then quickly hide her belongings. Until piece by piece she had gathered what she would need to make the twenty-three-mile journey into town. A dangerous trip for any local, especially for a city girl like her. How would she navigate under starless skies, through gator filled swamps, across a plain where every tree on every trail and dry path looked the same? Despair filled her heart and a tear fell from her eye. She quickly wiped it away and took a deep breath. She wanted to find out if Raquel was truly where Dr. Rutowski claimed she was or had she disappeared like the others?

The Widow Maker invented a twisted game down in the basement chamber in which he would bait his captives. Just when it appeared to be that some of the long-term occupants of the chamber to had figured out Dr. Rutowski's basic routines. The first step to master his timetable so they could escape. He abruptly changed something about his methodology that left them guessing again. Whether it was the order in which he retrieved them from their cells, or how long he left them unshackled and unattended with his back turned while he fetched some notes form the file cabinet about nine feet away by the wall opposite the staircase to his office. Sometimes he even left one of their cell doors open with his cellphone on the table. It never got reception down there in the chamber, but still he brought it to torture them and intentionally left it in plain sight while he fetched various instruments. This went on for several weeks. Little did they know that he was actually leading them on intentionally as a means of mental torture with false hope. Their own minds being suffocated by desperation blinded them from the truth that none of them would ever make it to the staircase alone. Each of them was in an extremely weakened physical state. This was due to severe dehydration and weeks without sunlight. They had been tortured in numerous ways and only one of them could actually walk. He had taken all of their shoes to hinder anyone from leaving. Not only was the partially excavated earthen floor callous with sharp rocks, but there were also scattered pieces of tiny bones from scores of rats that had been fed to them for protein that littered the floor. This made it very difficult for any barefooted individual to pass with ease.

The Widow Maker intentionally left open the door of one girl named Maria, to make her think he had gone upstairs for some urgent matter. Although he had never left and smiled at her from out of a dark corner, like a hunter trapping his prey. He watched as she slowly stuck her head out and peeked around. When she thought she had a clear path of escape into a storage room that contained a small ground level window. While she made her way toward the exit. Her eyes were wide as she looked around in fear. Chico Rivera mumbled after her as loud as he could through the coarse thread between his lips, "Maria, hurry up, get help. Please get me out of here."

Another patient told him to shut up. He persisted to mumble after her even louder. Maria looked around between his constant calls and imagined sounds for fear of being caught. She became distracted and punctured her foot on something sharp. She collapsed instantly with a thud and gently patted the bottom of her puss swollen, venomous infected feet until she found out what she had stepped on. She winced as she slowly pulled the tip of a long slender bone from between her blackened blood covered toes. The bone had bright red blood on it and looked like it had been part of a large rodent's spine. She quickly covered her mouth out of fear she had been heard by her captor. Then looking back at the doorway, she pulled herself into the storage room.

She saw a mixed pile of women and men's shoes from various abductees. Anxious to see her pink Converse tennis shoes under an open window to the outside. She quickly grabbed and tucked her shoes under her arm and tried to climb the steel wall using the soldered bolt tips to get up to the window. She quickly slipped and broke three of her toes. Agonized, she cried out in pain as she stared up at the dazzling beauty of the sun across an open field of freshly cut grass and trees. Suddenly the window began to close by the pull of a string that ran over the top of the door. Dry voiced she cried out, "No, wait!" The lock on the small thick window, that her frail body would have never fit through clicked as it shut tight. Maria looked and saw her shoes close by that she had dropped when she fell. Slowly, she cradled them to her chest and cried. Seconds later she noticed that her head was next to a pipe that was welded onto the floor. A clear, thick nauseous gas seeped out of it. It was then that she became aware of the warm temperature in the room. Alarmed, she realized the room she had crawled into actually was not a storage room at all. It was in reality an old incinerator room. When she turned and tried to crawl back out, she noticed Dr. Rutowski standing there. The Widow Maker tossed a lit match in the air and closed the door. While the match twirled in the air her thoughts twirled in her mind as to how she had been tricked. When the match hit the floor next to her head the glow of the flames ignited in her eyes. Her anguished scream filled the basement chamber and caused the others to try to hide in their compartments.

CHAPTER 11
COGNITIVE RECALIBRATION

———○⟨⟩○———

While Raquel lay on the floor in the dark of the quiet room all alone, soiled linens lay stockpiled in the corner next to her. After nearly nine hours had gone by without any bathroom privileges, she tried to sleep but no longer could hold it. So, she removed all the linen from the bed and erected a wall to contain her urine and stool in the corner. She felt so relieved afterward that she no longer cared about the smell that grew in the room. It was horrible like a slow draining puss-filled abscess. It wasn't long before a nauseous scent filled her clothes like a septic tank full of decomposing bile forgotten by a lake on a hot summer's day. Eventually she even tasted it in her mouth. So, she slept on the floor at the opposite end of the room for fresh air with her nose by the door.

Darkness filled the room twenty-four hours a day. Hours that went by without a sound that anyone else was nearby. She felt utterly helpless, cold, and alone. No longer able to escape the demons of bitterness that she had ran from since the slaughter of her loved ones. A highly charged vortex of her thoughts stole her away from the present darkness and back to a hurtful past.

Once again, she found herself naked and unsure how she got to the corner store. Her fingernails were caked with various meats. Strange symbols written in blood covered the glass window of the butcher's counter while an officer's flashlight examined her eyes for traces of coherent life. Raquel thought about how much she wanted her life back so that she could live for her daughter and grandchild. Light grew in her eyes as her mind slowly reset to reality. She beat her fist against the floor as the realization of where she was at and how much danger she was in took hold. She had seen past the mask of true darkness; its face would haunt her for life. She remembered the agonized cries that came through the bookcase in Dr. Rutowski's office during their one-on-one session, or had her many medications finally seized her mind? She had been known to talk to the walls, but now the walls seemed to talk back.

The shadow of a figure crossed the light under the door. A set of keys jingled outside. Raquel felt her heartbeat in her throat as fear gripped her mind. She ran and squatted in the far corner and put her hands up to hide her face as if by doing so they would somehow make her invisible. She balled up and screamed as the door opened, then an angelic voice that she had not heard in what appeared like a lifetime ago called out to her.

Nevaeh whispered into the darkness, "Raquel? Raquel, is that you?" Raquel peeked out from behind the shield of her hands that she hoped protected her well. Despite the stench that filled the room, Nevaeh ran towards her as tears fell from her eyes. Hysterical she repeated over and over again, "Oh my God! Oh my God!" Raquel arose quickly and stepped forward with clarity in her eyes. She had lost everything she cared about in broad daylight but rediscovered herself in darkness.

A tear fell from Nevaeh's eyes while she looked around the room and held Raquel's face in the palms of her hands Raquel made an attempt to beautify herself. She patted down her hair and wiped sleep from the corners of her eyes. Her voice was filled with grateful sobs as she said, "I'd hug you right now, but it would probably be better if I bathe first." Her gracious words and humble smile warmed Nevaeh's heart. Her voice though soft was empowered, refreshed, coherent. Nevaeh hugged Raquel tight as if at any moment she would somehow disappear. She thought how terrible of Dr. Rutowski to lock this poor woman away. Panic filled thoughts soon flooded her mind as she visualized Dr. Rutowski showing up at any second.

Neveah told Raquel, "Quick, follow me. We're getting

the hell out of here." Not knowing that the covers in the corner were filled with fecal matter, Nevaeh snatched the blanket to wrap around Raquel. Raquel yelled, "No, wait," as Nevaeh yanked the bedspread from the floor. One pop of the heavily soiled covers flung feces across the door and wall. Nevaeh vomited while Raquel embarrassingly stated, "I tried to warn you. What else was I supposed to do? I've been in this room three days without a bathroom." Nevaeh said, "You did what you had to do. Tell me, are you hurt? Can you walk?" Raquel quickly said, "I'm fine. Get me the hell out of here before he comes back."

Nevaeh wrapped her arm around Raquel, who put her hand up to block the blinding hall light from her sight. As they left, Nevaeh took a fork from a dirty food tray in the hall. She bent it in the lock to make it appear as if Raquel had escaped on her own using the utensil. Shortly after they had left, the sound of hard sole dress shoes approached from the opposite end of the corridor. As the footsteps neared the door, they became slow and purposeful in stride.

The Widow Maker heckled a dark quote as he came down the hall, "There once lived a reaper that made many to repent. Those unworthy of the light, darkness awaited them." While he twisted his dark tale suddenly his words tailed off. His eyes noticed the cracked door to the quiet room. When he pushed open the door Raquel was gone. He scoffed at the fork prop as an insult to his intelligence. Then he picked up a set of keys marked by a small charm representing Pandora's Box. Coldly he said, "Nevaeh, she has become quite the nuisance. It's imperative I shorten her leash. Taking fruit from my vineyard will not be tolerated. First, let me see what she has done with my star pupil."

An hour later Dr. Rutowski found Raquel sitting in group, closely under Nevaeh. She was bathed, her hair combed, and was clothed in her right mind. Quietly, he stood by the bookshelf and examined her. A peaceful look filled her eyes that said she had overcome the storm in her mind. The other patients marveled at her. The more he stared at her tranquil state the more his blood boiled. If there was anything more unnerving to the Widow Maker than a live witness it had to be a living convert. There had been far too many occasions to where he had seen that whole experience play out unfavorably for the torturer. History has proven time and time again that living converts are the most deadliest weapon against any regime. Their personal 'Road to Damascus' experience would never be enough. Eventually each one of them became a symbol of hope for others. Despite their many undeniable mental instabilities a few patients soon believed that they too could defeat the darkness like Raquel.

There was a loathsome look in the eyes of the Widow Maker as he studied Raquel with Nevaeh. How foolish of her to think that she could shed her past like skin and somehow be free from all her former snake-like ways. As she sat there and smiled no one in the room was wise to the fact that his intentions grew darker with each passing second. None, except Emily Frost, who smiled as if she herself was tightening the noose. She cradled a single thought in her mind like a sickly child born with the Ebola virus. One whose very breath had the power to kill everyone in the room. How would the next encounter between Raquel and Dr. Rutowski end? Would it end peacefully or painfully? Would the Dr. Jekyll, Mr. Hyde like mind of Dr. Rutowski bury the hatchet of her past infractions of the laws in his house or would he absolve his bitterness and bury a hatchet in her chest? She was certain by the look in his eyes as he wrote on a napkin, he was preparing a chilling epitaph for her headstone.

Two floors beneath the quiet group room where grateful glances fell upon Raquel, the mental strength of Chico Rivera quickly dissipated with each of his shallow breaths. The Widow Maker had tortured him now forty days and forty nights. Sorrow clung to him like thick sweat after a long journey under the desert sun. His back was a pin cushion of glass shards. Blood seeped from his eyes and ears as he became tone deaf and lost his mind. His thoughts were fragmented and jumbled. Tossed to and fro like flying debris under gale force winds in the eye of a storm.

Occasionally, he remembered brief fragments of life with his passive housewife. She was quiet, shy, and undemanding. She wore plain clothing, simple dresses, and was forgiving by nature. Untiringly she still passed out flyers about him missing every day though. He had treated her like shit over the past five years they were together. He never even gave her the cheap honeymoon he had promised her. He never took her on dates, helped her clean up, told her she was beautiful, spoke kindly to her or said thank you for anything she did. Such small sentiments were viewed by him as weakness. Now that he had begun to reap tremendously behind the seeds of ungratefulness he had sown, he missed her terribly. Although she deserved more, and her life was definitely better without him. She still fixed him a plate every meal and stared blank-faced across the table of their tiny kitchen and wept bitterly behind his disappearance.

The sound of footsteps could be heard descending into the lair. Slowly the image of his wife faded from his mind. Also, his hope of actually leaving that subterranean world of darkness beneath the floor of the asylum. The Widow Maker instantly scoffed at his tears when he rounded the corner. Callously he told him, "What seems to be the trouble? We haven't even begun today's exercises yet. Could it be that the turtle of your past mistakes has finally caught up with the rabbit lifestyle you thought you could live? Howbeit your dreams and conquests were in reality ephemeral, short-lived and rather foolish." While he spoke, Chico Rivera went into epileptic shock. The other captives stood at their cell doors horrified as he convulsed and vomited a thick white liquid on himself. Agitated by his weakness the Widow Maker headed into a side room as he mumbled, "Don't check out on me yet. The party is just getting started."

The rugged squeak of a cart's wheels could be heard being pushed back out of the room. The Widow Maker emerged with an old generator. He splintered a cable, tore a long piece of gray duct tape, and secured the cable to his chest. With several turns of the old hand crank generator, he revived his heart. Tiny vapors of smoke rose from Chico Rivera's charred flesh as he said, "Listen carefully my paragons of light. You are my patterns of perfection. I have given you true purpose. No one dies without my permission. Stop pretending your past transgressions have no sway over your future consequences. Nor allow yourselves to become fixated on me for eventually something brutal was bound to happen to you and to some of you that feel the terrors you've experienced should never happen to anyone. I say Never is here. As the harbinger of death, I've come to give you a time of absolution. A time to make penance before you cross over to the other side. Trust me, it would be far better for you to set your house in order on this side rather than the other. There are things shrewder than even I waiting to greet all with unbalanced books."

Though clothed in her right mind and back amongst the somewhat norm of society, Raquel sat and confided in Sam Green about how she felt as if she had just crossed a vast chasm of emotional distraught in search of reality and comfort only to be reminded as she emerged from the sweltering flames that nobody truly gave a damn either way. Her mental reserve of strength was dilapidated, wasted, ruined, destroyed.

That night as she dreamed, Raquel stood by a woodsy field where every tree was marked by a missing persons flyer of her face. At the far end of the field a dark figure dressed in all white twirled a scalpel in his hand. While he smiled hungrily at her from beneath is fedora-style brim, electrical surges coiled in his eyes like snakes in a pool of water. She turned to run and tripped over a stone. Slowly she fell towards the ground, hit the dirt hard and sat up in bed. She placed two fingers under her tongue, which revealed blood in her mouth. Confused by the dream and frightful, she gasped as a big pair of eyes by the bed blinked from someone there in the dark with her.

CHAPTER 12
MENTAL NOTES

A set of pearl white teeth glistened in the dark as they inched closer to Raquel. Terrified, she shook uncontrollably and started to scream. Nevaeh quickly turned on the bedside lamp just as Raquel swung her pillow in defense. Terror filled her eyes as they frantically searched the room. Nevaeh said, "You sounded like someone was killing you. Are you okay? What were you dreaming about?" All of Raquel's senses were heightened. She jumped at the sound of a loose shutter that knocked against the room window. Turning, she said, "I just had the most horrible dream ever." Nevaeh eased out of the chair she had curled up in and onto the bed next to Raquel. Her voice softened to a sympathetic whisper. She smiled encouragingly and said, "It's okay, you're safe. There's nobody else in here except for me."

Huge tears filled Raquel's eyes. Her voice cracked with several short gasps for air as she choked back heavy sobs. Vivid details filled her mind as she recalled the imagery of her dream. She looked down and cringed as she said, "You don't understand, it was all so real. I stood by this barren forest that had no sun or cloud patterns in the sky. A thick grayish-blue light, ice cold, seemed to pass through everything. Old white pieces of paper, with blurred pictures flapped on all the dry mold-covered tress. A nauseous feeling grew in me from the god-awful stench of puss-like maggots that saturated the soil. I stepped closer to one tree to see the face that was on the paper. I vomited for the picture on the tree was my face. I stumbled back in shock as the question crossed my mind. Whose face is on the other trees? I quickly ran to several trees and snatched the papers from them. One by one I flipped through the soiled sheets. I couldn't believe it; all the papers had my face on them. I looked up and there was suddenly an endless field of tress in front of me and all of them had the same white paper on them. That's when I noticed him step from behind a tree."

Raquel paused and looked Nevaeh in her eyes. Nevaeh grabbed her hand and said, "Its okay, I'm right here with you." Raquel began to stutter as one huge tear swelled up in her right eye and she struggled to speak. Nevaeh scooted closer to her and placed her arm around her. Raquel started to rock back and forth; her hands shook uncontrollably. A wild primal look filled her eyes as she said, "It was him. Although he wore an all-white suit and one of those fancy brimmed hats tilted over his face. I know it was him. His skin was living dead-like. The flesh over his left jaw was missing. I could sense death when he smiled at me. His eyes were unforgiving as fire, as cold and relentless as a lynching. With each step he took towards me my physical strength balled up and died. I knew then that if I didn't run it wouldn't be long before he did something dark to my soul.

Although I was a good distance away from him his movements seemed swift, cat-like as he darted between the trees. His strides grew longer as he lunged forward and disappeared behind one tree. Then he reappeared behind another tree several feet closer to me. Terrified, I screamed behind thoughts of being caught at any moment. I instantly became more focused on getting away than looking at where I was going. I turned, tripped, and fell." Raquel grabbed her head in agony and tasted the blood inside her mouth. She said, "What the hell," as she felt several other tender spots across her ribs and stomach. Then she asked Nevaeh, "How can this be? I thought it was all just one horrible dream, right?"

Nevaeh's eyes widened as she leaned in closer to Raquel and gently rubbed her back. She measured her next set of words carefully while she stared at Raquel, who stared at the blood on her fingertips, from inside her mouth. She said, "To some it may have been just another bad dream, but your mind has made the darkness real for you." Raquel asked, "What does that mean?"

Nevaeh responded, "Unfortunately it means that if you die in one of your dreams your mind may fully shut down and you die for real in life." Raquel slowly looked up and over at Nevaeh as she shivered and asked, "Why is this happening to me?" Nevaeh pulled Raquel's head onto her chest and slowly rocked her. Huge crocodile teardrops fell from her eyes while she whispered, "Shh, Its okay. You're not alone. You have to keep fighting. We can beat him. Even though he's cruel and capricious, he does not control our fate. I've got a plan to get you out of here." Raquel pushed back from Nevaeh, searched her eyes for truth and asked, "What about you?" Nevaeh softly placed her hand onto Raquel's cheek and said, "Don't worry about me. Just promise me that when the time comes you will help some of the others get out if you can? This started with me and him. It ends with me and him."

Raquel rebutted, "But Nevaeh." Neveah snapped back, "But nothing, Raquel. I need your help on this. It takes two people to open the security gate. I'll turn the key on the inside control panel. I need you to operate the control pad inside the guard booth and help lead the others to safety." Raquel asked, "are there other staff members that are going to help us?" Nevaeh said, "Right now its just us, but I'm working on recruiting others, like Sam Green, and maybe even Emily Frost."

Hysterical, Raquel said, "Emily? Are you crazy? She's probably more twisted than Dr. Rutowski." Nevaeh responded, "Look, I haven't figured out all the details. I just know we stand a better chance of surviving together than alone. Wait here. The sun will be up soon. I have to go do my normal rounds and check on the other patients. Put a chair on this door until you hear the orderlies in the hall handing out breakfast bags. I know you've had a tough night, but I need you to somehow pull it together. We have to avoid drawing any suspicion to ourselves. When the time comes you can spread the word at group or something to all who are able to leave." Nevaeh quickly wiped the sleep away from her clothing, eyes and brushed off her. Raquel asked, "Nevaeh, what did you mean by those able to leave?" Nevaeh said, "Let me be honest, I don't think everyone will make it out."

Nevaeh softly closed the room door and leaned her head against its cool surface. She took several slow, deep breaths to regain her composure. It had been an extremely long night of tossing and turning for her too. It would be an equally hellish day of stressors and mental outbursts. Only one question ran through her delicate mind. 'How long could she keep this up?' As of late she had starved her body of its proper nourishment. Daily her ravaged mind fought for peace. Caught off guard when she looked and saw Emily in her doorway, she cried, "Oh Shit! You scared the hell out of me." Emily asked, "Can you help me?" Nevaeh stared uncomfortably at her for a few seconds. Then she mumbled to herself, "What the bloody hell is she doing awake? It's far too early for her mind games." Emily's gaze on the other hand lowered at Nevaeh as if somehow, she was trying to decipher why she had just come out of Raquel's room this early in the morning. Nevaeh took a long deep breath and asked, "Sure, what is it, Emily?" Emily peered at her as if looking into her soul. She asked, "Where's Raquel? Is she okay? She must be having trouble sleeping since you watched her all night. Nevaeh stated plainly, "She's fine. What do you need? I have rounds to make."

Emily's vocal façade offset by an investigative eye deepened as she asked, "Can I have a sleep over too? Oh, I'd like that. I'm a good listener." To end the conversation Nevaeh said, "We can look into that later. First, I would need to know who the individual is and what accommodations they may need. Plus, due to medication requirements it probably wouldn't be an all nighter." Nevaeh turned to walk off. Emily said, "Ms. Sharai, I have somebody in mind already." Nevaeh stopped and mumbled to herself, "who in their right mind (if that's appropriate in this setting) would stay overnight in a room with her?" Then she asked aloud, "Who is it Emily?" With a clear voice unlike anything she had ever heard from her, Emily said, "You. I believe you and I have some things we need to discuss. Let's be clear, Ms. Sharai, unless you want to become a private guest in the chamber downstairs you will need to implore my help." Nevaeh said, "What are you talking about Emily?"

Suddenly the sound of a heavy object could be heard being pushed from blocking the door of a patient's room. Nevaeh glanced in the direction of the sound as sleepy-eyed Sam Green asked, "Is it breakfast time yet?" Nevaeh looked down at her watch and replied softly, "No not yet Sam, but orderlies should be around here in about another twenty minutes." Sam did not reply. He just closed his door and put the dresser back. When Nevaeh looked up Emily was gone from her doorway. The sound of her repeatedly singing the title "Three Blind Mice" drifted from her room and down the hall. Nevaeh thought briefly about going in there, but she was already running late that morning. Plus, there were a hundred and one things that she needed to do. Starting with a welfare check on the other patients. Plus, figure out how to quickly reduce and supplement all of Dr. Rutowski's individual therapy sessions. This was to try to eliminate the risk of any more patients coming up missing on her watch. More importantly given the increased disturbances of Dr. Rutowski's psychosis. There were two things that had to become imperative that she must do immediately. First and foremost, she needed to call the homes of every student that came for the internship tour to check and see if they actually made it back home. Secondly, work out all the kinks in her escape plan. To get herself and as many others as possible out.

Nevaeh could no longer trust the word of Dr. Rutowski. His dark schizothymic psychosis had taken him way to far off the reservation. She knew that he had falsified guests logs, patient records and even several court documents. All to advance his own personal agenda. Time froze as her mind coasted like a car down a desert highway and stalled at an obscure thought. A thought that made her cringe. She realized that all his heinous acts she had discovered, and they were many, were just the tip of the iceberg. The majority of his destructive acts lay hidden beneath the murky waters of deception. He was a highly skilled chess player. Each move he made was cold and calculated. Part of his design was to bait and eliminate everyone, especially those his dark psychosis told him stood in opposition to their objectives.

This is all she constantly thought about. While she headed towards the personal wing that only she and Dr. Rutowski live on. The housing wing itself was quiet. There appeared to be no sign of him anywhere. This helped to ease her nerves tremendously. She understood that time was not on her side. That she only had a few moments before Dr. Rutowski returned. She also knew that seeing him was inevitable. They were both isolated on the same compound, a compound that he had turned into a coffin. Still, she prayed that whenever she saw him at any point during the course of the day, that they would be in a room with others. Navaeh thought about her own safety and to not take any chances of being caught on the wing by him. So, she quickly removed her three-inch heels and tiptoed barefoot down the hall. Cautiously she pressed her ear against the door of every room she passed. Her heartbeat increased with every step she took. Meanwhile, she double checked the hall in front of her and behind her. When she reached her room, she inched the door open and peeked inside. It was empty. Once inside she quickly changed clothes. She filled up a bag with all the cash she had, plus several personal effects. She raced over to the end table and dumped the contents of the drawer on the bed. She said, "Perfect!" Then lifted an old ring of skeleton keys. This gave her access to multiple rooms inside the original house. She ruffled her bed sheets to make it look like she had slept there. Then she quietly went to go stash her bag.

Chapter 13
Dark Frost

I t was almost 9:30 am and there was no indication that Dr. Rutowski would show for the morning group. Only five of his original twelve patients committed to the asylum sat in attendance. With the fast approach of lunch, staff dismissed them back to their rooms. Emily Frost was the only patient that remained behind. Quietly she sat and stared out the bay window at the cold unforgiving sea. The waters raged violently under cloven skies scared by thick patches of darkness. Rarely had the staff seen Emily like this. Her face chiseled by distortion. Her patchy eyebrows perfectly flared by thought. Slowly her eyelids lowered and shrouded her vision in darkness. Her mind transfixed on the distant dark memories of her childhood tortures. The children in her neighborhood that made fun of her

Downs Syndrome.

Her mind shifted to the last memory of her mother, Amanda Frost. Drunken, she lay half naked on the couch. The landlord walked in to evict her, but soon found himself renegotiating her tenancy in exchange for sensual pleasure. Why had life been so cruel to her, abandoned her and given her a mother who treated her like a blight against nature? Amanda Frost cherished her own physical beauty so much that she felt embarrassed to be seen with Emily in public. Embittered, she blamed Emily when the male lovers half her age did not stick around. Emily Frost's inner cry for love and affection gradually became a desire for hate and vengeance. Now, at the asylum, she sat in the quietness of solitude, beneath the window. The well-oiled machinery of her mind rusted at one malicious thought, find Dr. Rutowski, convince him to let her be his apprentice by telling of the fictitious alliance with Nevaeh Sharai. That she does not savor the things he is apt to teach.

Quietly Emily stood up from her chair and walked with the graceful posture of a ballet dancer over to the window. While she stood there lost in thoughts as tumultuous as the waters of the Gulf of Mexico, she heard a clear interrupting cough behind her. Immediately on impulse she buckled at her knees and acted as if she were afflicted with Parkinson's disease and about to collapse. Sam Green said, "I must admit you are a very talented liar. The likes of which I haven't seen since I was swimming with the government sharks and private contractors while I was still active duty on tour in Afghanistan. Very impressive, but there's no need for that with me."

Slowly Emily straightened up and turned her head just enough to reveal a cold calculated methodical stare, out of the corner of her right eye. When she spoke, there was not a single trace of frailty in her voice. Sam knew that she was a master of masquerades. He had witnessed her instantly change her facial expression. She readily displayed an ability to alter her physical appearance to make it appear as if she suffered from a chronic illness like Multiple Sclerosis. Additionally, he had never heard her natural voice, which was like that of a highly respected educators and crisp as the winter air. She said, "Why Sam, you speak of Afghanistan as if you're still at war. Tirelessly you have devoted yourself to doing recon on me and for what? But to try to score some points with a flawed system that has clearly forgotten that you even exist?"

Sam lowered his head like a cowering antelope that had accidently stumbled across a lion. A glass-like stare filled his eyes. Memories flooded his mind of being pinned down, under enemy gunfire. Next, of him being honored with combat medals of valor. Then a candlelight dinner with his wife. Her tired, worried eyes monitored their sick son in her lap. Sam flinched in regret as blood-soaked, feathered book pages fell like huge snowflakes to the living room floor. Then the bodies of his wife and toddler son with wax smooth faces collapsed in the living room chair. A rifle fell to the floor at his side.

While inside the delusion, Sam had not noticed that Emily had left the window. She quietly stood over him and observed his delusional revisiting of the past. Emily smiled smugly as she smacked the table to gain his full attention. Startled, he snapped out of the trance as she said, "There you are little mouse. Still chasing that coveted piece of cheese in your mind that you once called family and life? Don't worry, that will soon come to an end once your time comes to visit with the doctor. We're all on his list, that's why we're here. Haven't you solved his riddle yet?"

Sam asked, "What riddle?"

Emily turned and walked back toward the window as she recited, "The first day of life is much like the last, you come and go alone. Light shines through the doorway of darkness and who truly understands it? Of all the possible thresholds to cross you've been chosen for this one. Death, the ambassador of a dying world waits as a willing escort to guide. Will, is an illusion of the mind within the grand design of true life. Come, drink from the cup of destruction, it beckons all flesh."

Sam shouted, "That same dark passage has been stuck in my head for days now. What is that? Where do I know that from?"

Emily retorted, "You've heard it in group you idiot. It's his cryptogram and a warning to us. Now see that right there is the problem. The few souls that still roam these convalescent halls. You float around in a miasma of mild hypnosis looking for salvation in the form of a pill from the hand of someone more mentally disturbed than you yourselves."

Sam retorted, "Don't insult me Emily, like you possess some far greater mind to be paid homage to. For if you were truly as smart as you think you are, you wouldn't be here with the rest of us now, would you?"

Emily's glance shot cold toward him as if in her mind she had just ripped his heart right out of his chest. While she walked back to the window she mumbled under her breath, "Why, you loathsome parasite, I'd love to add you to my bucket list of lives to destroy, but you have no life."

Sam asked again, "So what is it, Emily? What's the point of his allegory?"

Emily stared out the window and said, "Dr. Rutowski is plagued with a schizothymic disorder that's literally like having another soul in his body. The allegory tells us the new mission and title of his life. His mission is twofold. First, he wants to establish a legacy that serves as the ultimate and final warning to all, especially to those that think they can continue to live without regard of no man, receive no recompense in this life and repeatedly cheat death. Secondly, his title, 'Lux Ab Exitium Velle Venere' is in actuality the personification of his true nature to teach penance. The origin is from the Latin and translates as 'The Light of Death Will

Come.' This implies a journey of walking to and fro without destination like the fallen angel in the book of Job, Chapter one. The real question is what incident drove him to this path and who's next on it?"

Knowing that Emily was prone to play games, Sam dryly said, "So what are you saying my next one on one session with Dr. Rutowski will be my last?"

Emily's voice lowered almost to a whisper as she said, "No offense, but I'm surprised that he has kept you around this long. I'm quite certain he has devised a systematic approach to the disposal of his rather unique clients. The rarest of cases and in some respects the most troubled or hopeless. You, however, don't really fit the uncommon profile of this caseload. For although tragic, your situation is more prevalent among former military personnel than most realize."

Sam stood up from the table. He thought about the towering stature of Dr. Rutowski; at six feet four inches tall he was agile and quiet like a cat. Often times he had practically appeared out of nowhere, just standing right next to him as if he had simply walked through the wall. It was unnerving how he did that. Why didn't Dr. Rutowski announce himself when he approached someone like a normal person? The more he listened to the thorned words from the morally withered rose of Emily's mind, the more it all made sense to him. His thoughts fogged behind the high dosage of medication he was on. His strength vanished and he felt dizziness overtake him. He tried to focus on his military and police training. He realized there was only one way he could survive this nightmare. He had to stop taking that medication. He sensed everything that was happening was leading up to something much worse. He had to be ready when that time came. He needed his mind clear in order to do that. He was confident that if push came to shove, he could handle himself fairly well. He was not so optimistic about the other patients.

Sam eyed Emily curiously while she stared out the window. He walked over, leaned his back against the glass and said, "You know you're wrong about one thing."

Emily looked at him out of the corner of her eye and said, "Oh, I seriously doubt that, but please enlighten me."

Sam walked past Emily and whispered closely by her ear, "There's another anomaly at this asylum. A flaw in his delicate design that I'll bet he didn't count on. That anomaly is you."

Emily's eyes flared momentarily then relaxed as she looked away. Sam continued, "So what's your end game? How do you survive all of this?"

A dark smile formed on Emily's face as her keen sense of hearing picked up the faint sound of staff coming down the hall. Sam was completely unaware they were approaching. He repeated, "What is it, Emily? I know that twisted little mind of yours has plotted something."

Emily softly said, "Oh, there's no need to plot. I already have an exit strategy. Come closer and I'll tell you."

Sam stepped closer and leaned in towards Emily just as staff rounded the corner. Emily said, "You're my ticket out of here."

Suddenly, she contorted her body like a frail child and collapsed into him. Sam quickly wrapped his arms around her to prevent her from falling. Staff turned the corner, saw him, and immediately yelled, "Sam, let go of her!"

Sam pleaded, "Wait, you don't understand. I was helping her. She was about to fall."

Staff replied, "Sure thing, whatever you say. Just let her go."

Sam looked at Emily and said, "Why you dirty, conniving, manipulative, little bitch. I ought to…"

Emily turned her head toward staff and asked, "Can you help me?"

Staff rushed Sam, who became enraged and threw Emily to the floor. He broke down in a defensive stance as Emily hit the floor with a thud. Realizing what he had done he quickly squatted to try to help her up. The spear-like tackle from staff quickly changed his feeling of compassion to pure adrenaline. Instinctively he wrapped up one staff in a choke hold and kicked the other guard in his kneecap to take him out. The guard in the choke hold hit the emergency body response button on his radio to alert additional staff. Within less than a minute multiple staff members flooded the room. One of them yelled, "Hold him down" and produced a small leather case that contained two hypodermic needles filled with 300 cc's of tranquilizer. After administering the first shot, Sam was still difficult to restrain, so the second shot was delivered. Fifteen seconds later Sam's body had slowed to a twitch. He drooled heavily while he mumbled and tried to warn staff about Emily. She had been helped back into her chair and received first aid to a small cut above her right eye. While staff dragged Sam out of the room. Once again, Emily stared icily out of the window at the cold unforgiving waters of the Gulf of Mexico like he did not even exist. His grumbling grew fainter as he was carried to an isolation room down the hall.

Meanwhile, Emily exhaled deeply through tightly pursed lips. Her mind forcefully crawled back to a scene in her childhood home. A donated mattress sat on the floor of her bedroom. All her clothing balled up in a small black plastic garbage bag on the floor. Several outdated toys from the thrift store were flung across her bed. Her mother lay half naked on the couch in a drunken stupor. Emily peeked out through her cracked bedroom door at an unknown man who adjusted his clothes before he left. She turned and looked at her small, deformed stature in the tall broken mirror. A tear fell from her eye as she looked back at her mother and closed her bedroom door.

CHAPTER 14
WORKER BEES

N
evaeh tiptoed behind Dr. Rutowski from a safe distance as he headed into an old wing of the main house. Panic seized her mind behind thoughts of being discovered by him. Though she was a full hallway's length away. She felt paranoid and repeatedly jumped at the sound of each random creek of loose floorboards that were spread throughout the hall. Suddenly Dr. Rutowski stopped dead in his tracks. He looked back over his shoulder as though he had somehow sensed somebody was there. Nevaeh flung her body flat against the wall, around the corner and held her breath.

He saw no one there and continued down the hall until he reached a thick black, iron tempered door. A heavy crank type lever controlled the lock mechanism at its center. A small opening for a skeleton key was in the center of the crank. She watched as he removed a key, hidden beneath his shirt, fastened to a string that hung around his neck. She heard him speak to someone as soon as the door was open. Slowly he stepped inside the room and left the door open behind him. Nevaeh inched closer toward the sounds of multiple voices that came from inside the room. Obscure thoughts of horrid possibilities crawled across Nevaeh's mind like the tentacled legs of worker bees in a hive. She knew someone else was in there with Dr. Rutowski, but who? She removed her four-inch heals to avoid making any sound at all. When she was close enough, she slowly squatted and peeked around the corner of the hallway. She saw the five college interns that she had suspected had never left the asylum. She gasped out of fear for them.

Dr. Rutowski, who still had his back to the door, violently twisted in a demented form and snatched the glasses from his face. Terror filled the eyes of one girl. She jumped behind his contortion and curled up in the corner with her backpack. The girl next to her in Gothic style clothing and thick black makeup sat stone faced like an apprentice hoping to learn the secrets of the dark arts. Dr. Rutowski spoke in a low measured, wrathful voice completely different from his own. When Nevaeh leaned in to try to clearly hear what he said. She did not notice the rusted nail protruding through the floorboard. The nail easily punctured through her soft skin on an angle and its curved tip hooked deep into her tender flesh. Pain shot through her hand as she quickly whispered, "Ouch!"

The Widow Maker's head whipped toward the open doorway as Nevaeh yanked her hand from the floor and ducked back around the corner. Hot blood quickly dripped from the palm of her hand as she examined the small hole. She made a tight fist to slow the flow of blood. Upon hearing Dr. Rutowski make his way toward the door she jumped up and took off down the hall. He heard the fleeing footsteps as he reached the corner of the hallway. When he looked, he saw no one and was about to look further until he noticed the red droplets on the floor. He stooped down, dabbed the liquid with a finger and smelled it. He whispered, "Blood," through his teeth.

Meanwhile, the small footsteps of Nevaeh made haste down the hall. The Widow Maker stood and said, "I'll see you soon." Then he turned and walked back into the room. Now in the doorway his visage twisted again, and his expression softened. Dr. Rutowski removed his glasses from the pocket of his white lab coat along with a handkerchief from his back pocket. While he polished the lenses of his glasses he said, "A most pressing matter has come to my attention that I need to tend to at once. I'm afraid that we will have to finish our lecture at a later time." He waved goodbye to them, secured the door, and draped the key back around his neck. He whistled, "Three Blind Mice" as he headed down the hall.

Before he had reached his private wing an orderly approached, walking swiftly and half out of breath. Sensing something extreme had happened, Dr. Rutowski asked him, "What is it?" the orderly said, "Dr. Rutowski sir, I'm glad I found you. There was a serious incident involving two of the most unlikely to quarrel patients."

Dr. Rutowski folded his arms across his chest and looked sternly across the top of his glasses at the orderly. He asked, "This incident, was it a unified effort in an attempt to escape this facility?"

The orderly thought it was quite odd that Dr. Rutowski drew suspicion to residents plotting to escape. Quickly he shrugged off the comment and said, "No escapees sir. However, this matter was very alarming and came out of nowhere."

Dr. Rutowski snapped irritatedly and said, "Where is Ms. Sharai? Could she not deal with this? I have other pressing matters to deal with."

The orderly swallowed dryly and said, "I have not been able to locate Ms. Sharai since the morning group."

Dr. Rutowski thought suspiciously, 'Where is she?' but said, "Very well, what happened?"

The orderly said, "After the morning group the patients returned to their rooms for lunch. Only one patient remained behind, Emily Frost. When I returned, she was with Sam Green."

Dr. Rutowski interjected, "Staring out the bay

window at the gulf is her personal aid to embracing the darkness of her childhood memories. Why was Emily alone with Sam Green?"

The orderly said, "That's still unclear, but we had to sedate and place him in isolation. He became physically aggressive towards staff. He even slammed Emily to the floor. We were able to restrain him before any serious harm was done."

Dr. Rutowski said, "Good" turned and walked off. Halfway down the hall he spoke disturbingly to himself, "Still fighting for attention amongst yourselves. While you've lived like the woman at the well. All you've thirsted for in this life no matter how beautiful it has appeared it has been unable to satisfy you. For it has not been true life, but in reality, a mere reflection of death. For everything in this world is dying. Be it pleasure, entertainment, money, or power. Foolishly you have worshipped vanity hoping to find life, not knowing that you've been seeking death. Well, there's no longer any need to aimlessly seek death for death himself has come."

The all-white room that Sam Green had been reassigned to, had been carefully designed for long term patient safety. Each of the walls were heavily insulated by thick beanbag-like pads. They covered the entirety of the ceiling, floor, and walls. Only a small twelve by twelve-inch window with mirror coating was unpadded on the door. Except for the door, the pads were reinforced tightly at the individual boarders and sewn together by a coarse double stitched thread. The thread was made of a chemical mixture of hemp rope and plastic sealed within the walls. This converted the fabric into one giant canvas that snugly fitted inside the room like a bone deep inside muscled tissue. A continual hum of compressed recycled air was steadily vacuumed from inside the room. This eliminated any potential sound from a disgruntled guest to escape into the hall. It also prevented any sound from a passerby to disturb the time of reflecting within it. Unlike most padded rooms, this one was complete with several modest furnishings for minimal comfort. There was a small desk and twin-size bed inside the room that had been bolted to the floor. Two small shelves next to an intercom box held a couple of soft cover books. A bible sat on the nightstand by the bed. An adult size port-a-potty chair with water tank was positioned in the corner opposite the door. A 150-watt light bulb burned steadily from above.

When Dr. Rutowski arrived at the door he presumed that Sam Green would be unconscious behind effects of the tranquilizer shot rendered by staff. He was amazed to discover that Sam Green sat alert on the edge of the bed. He was completely naked in a suicide watch turtle suit. A standard protocol for high-risk patients. Woozy, he scooted to the edge of the bed and placed his head in the palms of his hands. Slowly he stood and stretched as if he had just awakened from a nap. He paced back and forth across the floor from padded wall to padded wall. The mirror reflection film that covered the small window on the door prevented him from noticing Dr. Rutowski's piercing gaze on the other side. Dr. Rutowski was about to press the intercom button outside the room to communicate with Sam on the inside. He quickly decided against it and to leave Sam be for now. He was not going anywhere anytime soon, plus there were more pressing matters at hand. Emily's side of the story would certainly be far more interesting than what Sam had to offer. Dr. Rutowski knew she had baited or provoked him in some kind of way, but how and why?

Inside the room Sam had come to the same conclusion about Emily and his extended stay. He thought to himself that at least for now he did not need to worry about any deadly appointment with Dr. Rutowski. If what Emily had said was true in any way? He was safe for now. He also knew that the best time to sort out things was after a good night's sleep. He tried to unwind by reading a little. He walked over to the shelf and grabbed the two soft cover books left behind. He hoped he would find a really good story to escape into for the meantime. He read aloud the title of the first book he grabbed from the shelf, "The Widow Maker Trilogy. Collector's Edition. The Awakening, The Rise and The Legend by Zoez Lajoune. A psychological thriller in which the inevitable yearnings of the human soul to survive are revealed. Man, this one sounds really good. I'd better save this one for the long haul over a couple of days just in case I'm still stuck in here." Then he grabbed the second book from the shelf and read the title aloud while heading over to the bed, "Alien Virus Love Disaster, stories by Abbey Mei Otis. There might be a good short story in here that I can unwind with." Just as he sat down on the bed two orderlies came, opened the door, and tossed him a bag lunch inside and a set of bedsheets. Sam yelled as they were closing the door, "Hey, I want to see Nevaeh. I didn't do anything wrong. This is really a big misunderstanding."

One of the orderlies responded, "Dr. Rutowski has been made aware of your reassignment to specialized housing. I'm sure either him or Ms. Sharai will be along soon as their schedule permits. If I see her, I will let her know you requested to speak with her."

Sam said, "Thank you. Will you please tell staff I apologize for earlier?" The staff member nodded yes and closed the door.

When Dr. Rutowski found Emily, she was back in her room on the secure patient wing sitting in her custom-made wheelchair. It's mahogany woodgrain trim around the soft well-oiled leather cushions had exquisite engravings. A flat touchscreen control pad was positioned beneath her right palm. It's high-tech sensory program only required the delicate touch of a finger to trace operate the movements of the chair. For such technology, the total cost had surged well above a pretty penny. Some say that the funds for her wheelchair had been comprised from many gullible humanitarians.

That after they made sizeable donations to aid in her longer healthcare, Emily killed them out of fear and bitterness that they too would now discard her like her mother Amanda Frost had done.

While Dr. Rutowski headed down the hall he contemplated the circle of life. That no matter what light you strive to experience eventually the darkness comes again. When he turned the corner into the residential hall several patients that noticed him scattered immediately. His intense stride carried a pressurized force in front of him that parted the cluster of their legs and swiftly created a pathway to Emily's room. Quickly they scattered like a colony of meddlesome roaches when the kitchen light is turned on in the middle of the night. Though Emily's words dripped as if from a hive of toxic honey sweet to the taste and smoother than oil, the end of them was like wormwood, sharp as a two-edged sword. Still, he longed to taste the sweet nectar of the rose which is her psyche. He drooled as he relished the thoughts of draining the life force from her and watching her fall like a dead pedal to the ground.

Part 3: Epitaph of Souls

CHAPTER 15
EXTERMINATION OF THE SURPLUS

D r. Rutowski stood in the doorway of Emily's
room. His frame towered and blocked most
of the hallway's light. The shadow of his
body dramatically darkened the Grimm Brothers short
story book she held in her hands. Although he did not
speak at first, she could tell it was him as she studied
the movements of the silhouette cast across her lap.
She watched as he removed the glasses from his face
along with a handkerchief from his back pocket. When
silence became unnerving Emily's usual theatrical
performance kicked in automatically. She was all sobs
while she shared her unfortunate plight. Dr. Rutowski
let her know immediately that he shared absolutely
no empathy toward her predicament. He only desired
to know the mechanics of what took place so that he

might discover the true motives and snatch the blanket off her plot.

While she carried on, she switched conversational topics several times. These covered everything from her lack of menstrual cycle to current medication. While she mindlessly babbled to try to distract him from the purpose of his visit, Dr. Rutowski began to hear the familiar chime of six nickels falling to the ground as his vision grew hazy. Emily looked up towards the door just as he began to slowly salivate like a hungry wolf. The Widow Maker smiled deathly at her. Then he cut her off mid-sentence and interjected, "Why Ms. Frost, let me be rather frank with you about one thing. If we're to make any true progress at all. There's no need to try to adorn an impudent mask with me and play the confused victim role for I already have a thorough list of the horrible secrets that exist between you, God, the devil, and the dead. Secrets darker than the deeds of Thomas Malthus the exterminator of the poor and disadvantaged. He used several of the deadliest killing illnesses and pathologies like COVID 19 to systematically eliminate the poor. While under the cloak of a concerned business representative of the private sector.

I also know that from your mother's womb to this asylum your life has been one long holocaust. A story of which the words were written with a quill pen, dipped in the blood of your victims. You too suffered in the wake of it but fear not o'child of great wickedness. A greater destruction like the atom bomb has come to liberate mankind from his terrible plight. Me, the Light of Death Himself, your nemesis the Widow Maker."

The Widow Maker paused as the smile widened on his face, then he walked over and stood uncomfortably close to her. This made her feel the threat of the moment. She braced herself as horrible fears crawled across her mind. Fears that told her she deserved everything she was about to get. The Widow Maker leaned in closely to her ear and said, "You know, Ms. Frost, I personally despise those that use a cloak to hide their true objectives. Those that never give their prey a fighting chance. Tell me, Ms. Frost, what was the real reason you used Sam Green as bait, or should I say as a distraction when staff approached? Had he discovered some truth about you buried alongside the ten miles of mommy issues that you so faithfully adorn as a mask?"

Emily said nothing. She knew perfectly well that, "Real knowledge is knowing what you don't know" -Confucius- By this time she understood that sometimes its best to just shut the hell up. With one hand he slowly started to reach for his back pocket where he kept the chloroform dipped cloth at and said, "Transgressions in my house. Why you fool I could destroy you at the speed of thought." Slowly he placed two fingers beneath Emily's chin and lifted her from her chair. Piercingly he stared into the corner of her dark chocolate eyes as if looking into her soul. His voice inflexion was sharp and dense as if coming through a wall when he said, "I could easily snatch the life force of out you."

Emily stared ahead and did not say a word. Just as he wrapped his cold hand around her face to cover her mouth. A staff member appeared in the doorway and said, "Um, excuse me, Dr. Rutowski sir." Slowly he turned his head to the door and said, "What is it? I'm in the middle of a session."

The orderly said, "I'm terribly sorry to interrupt you, but Ms. Sharai asked me to find you. She said she needs to speak with you about an urgent matter."

The Widow Maker turned his head, squinted his eyes, growled lowly like a building storm, and asked, "Where is she now?"

The orderly responded, "On her way to your office sir."

Immediately upon hearing that the Widow Maker's expression changed his thoughts shifted to her possibly discovering his demented creation, The Chamber. The orderly quickly walked off toward two arguing patients.

Dr. Rutowski's body slightly contorted and relinquished the Widow Maker's spirit. His hand ached as it left Emily's mouth. Slowly he stepped backwards to the door. He stood there momentarily until she looked sheepishly at him. It was then he sensed the intentions of the Widow Maker soften towards her. Had the lion come to respect the lamb?

Thirteen white boxes meticulously lined individual plastic braces protruding from the wall adjacent the bookshelf that covered the staircase to the chamber.

At first glance nothing appeared to have been touched. He knew if she had discovered the stairwell emergency sirens would be ablaze by now. Slowly, carefully like a child counting every Lego in the box he began to comb through the files on his desk. He sensed something had been taken, but what? Then he noticed the empty spot on his desk, next to a sealed glass jar. The jar contained the skeleton of an abnormally large rodent. "The journal!" He exclaimed as his blood quickly boiled. Enraged, he turned to the door to go and find Nevaeh. That's when he noticed that several of the white boxes had been moved out of their places. The lids on two of the boxes were still open and sat crooked on their shelves. Slowly he reached up and grabbed the first open box.

When he looked inside the ball joint plucked from Chico Rivera's leg glistened. He grunted, "Hmm." Then he closed the lid and sat it back on its shelf. Slowly, he lifted the last open box and looked inside at the crushed help bell from old man Stonewall's wheelchair. His mind shifted instantly to how the Widow Maker had taken old man Stonewall out to the woodshed early in the morning, just before dawn. As soon as the cock crowed, he severed his head with an axe. Slowly he began to hear the familiar chime of six nickels falling to the ground as his vision grew hazy. The Widow Maker spoke in a mocking voice, "Tsk, tsk, tsk still slow to believe that Nevaeh is a problem? Haven't you realized yet. . . a house divided against itself cannot stand?"

Dr. Rutowski mumbled to himself, "I never thought

that she would interfere like this." Enraged, the Widow Maker snapped back, "Enough! Yield to me!"

With every step that Dr. Rutowski took down the hall his mind was pulled further down a cankerous trail of memories. Each distorted projection cast itself on the wall in front of him and revealed the fate of a particular victim. Select ones whom he had slaughtered and kept a small token about. Often at night he relived each encounter. Mentally he tasted it, coveted it, until his mind craved it and it consumed him. Huge, bright, gold Latin phrases and obscure markings appeared on the walls in the hallway like hieroglyphs guarding his demented secrets of the past. With the slightest touch of either object that he pulled from its white box he was there again severing a person's head, giving them an injection of hydrochloric acid, or placing six highly polished nickels into their eyes. He shook his head to remove the intrusive images from his sight that quickly accumulated like overlapping chards on a table. The more the images compiled on the walls the darker his intentions grew towards Nevaeh Sharai. By the time he reached the end of the corridor, one thing had become imperative. The Widow Maker and he had become unified in a single thought. Kill Nevaeh Sharai as soon as they found her. Then place her body in the septic tank for the sewer rats to feast on. The time had come for her to give an account to the Reaper and prepare herself to meet the Boatman Charon. Nevaeh had violated their trust, and nothing would change their mind about her fate.

Dr. Rutowski quickly made his way back to the secure patient wing. One by one he checked every room. Time slowed to a crawl when he glanced inside Emily Frost's room. She locked eyes with him for a brief moment as he passed by. He noticed she had not moved a single inch from the spot the Dark One had left her at. Her worst sensations coursed through her skin like a mutating virus attacking its host. A sickening feeling paralyzed her muscles, even worse her thoughts. She'd shown weakness and felt extremely embarrassed behind it. After all, every person that had ever set themselves above her and tried to make her feel inferior. She had put all of them in their place. It began with her mother. She was supposed to protect her. Instead, she had treated her worst than Herodias did her naïve daughter in the biblical account. She used her daughter's innocence to seduce her drunk ex-husband's brother, who probably killed him so he could have her. All to gain the head of John the Baptist on a platter. Who spoke publicly against them?

Emily's mother made a profit off her Downs Syndrome daily. Her coveted prize was the solidarity attention of a younger man she barely knew and a knockoff Coach purse. Emily did not let her get away with it either. If she, had it her way neither would Dr. Rutowski. How could she let him talk to her like that? Then she remembered why. She remembered the magnetic force of darkness in his eyes. It seemed to pull her soul close to a spiritual abyss. She had done nothing because she could do nothing. She knew she needed a Plan B. Sam Green would have been a suitable option, but he was not a factor anymore. That only left her with one option, Nevaeh Sharai. But if Nevaeh did not survive this asylum who would tell her story?

Emily closed the door to her room and headed over to the closet. She grabbed her intake box from the shelf and removed an old Bible from it. It was the only meaningful item her mother had ever given her. She remembered how her mother often used it to hide money. A precautionary measure against some guests that had sticky fingers. Emily sat down and carefully peeled apart the crusted pages to Genesis Chapter 1. Then like God, she began to record her own story in the inner margins between each page.

The empty family wing of the house offered no true refuge for Nevaeh. The rooms were primarily empty and still required significant repairs. She paced back and forth in one room while she desperately flipped through several pages of the journal. Had this journal come from Carlos MacIntyre who was once Dr. Rutowski's patient? She felt shocked behind all that she had seen in Dr. Rutowski's office. Still, none of that compared to each detailed, methodical account chronicled on the feathered pages of the journal. A brief thought crossed her mind. If she made it out of this hell hole this would be her proof of the psychosis of Dr. Rutowski and what led to the inner workings of the asylum. Suddenly

Nevaeh heard footsteps approach. With nowhere to go she dropped and crawled through a small hole of broken boards in the wall of the closet. She sat there within the confines of the crawl space in between the walls and listened to Dr. Rutowski enter the room. Time was not on her side, because their next encounter was inevitable. Her reflection darkened as she powered down her iPhone to avoid being detected. Terrified, she squatted and covered her mouth. Quietly she listened to him search the room. Enraged he cried out as he violently ripped boards from the walls, "Nevaeh you test my patience with this game of cat-n-mouse. I do not wish to harm you. I just want you to GIVE BACK THE JOURNAL!" Nevaeh said nothing. Then she took off running as he tore through the adjacent wall and looked into the crawl space for her. He heard her footsteps and quickly yelled at the other wall, while following her pace, "GIVE US BACK THE JOURNAL!" Neveah continued on and ran faster. She knew that she had crossed the line by stealing the journal from his desk and tampering with those thirteen small, white boxes in his office.

CHAPTER 16
WITHERED FLESH

here are places to go to beyond truth's protective barriers. Dark places that defy logic and go far beyond belief. Among these mysteries is a cold fact. Out of all the deadly pathogens that Mankind like David has defeated with his slingshot of technology, there is yet a giant like Goliath that stands on the battlefield of destiny he has yet to face. His name is Chronos, Greek for time. He is the number one killer in the cosmos and has set an appointment to face each one of us on any terms. He doesn't flinch at the rules of engagement. Be it tragic accident, reckless lifestyle, old age, birth defect or one of his favorites the common cold. That suddenly cripples the immune system and shuts down every major organ of the body in a single night.

He has operated viscously, systematically, unchangeably long before there was man. He has marked all the seasons upon the earth with conditions that no matter where one constructs a dwelling all things present there are destined to wither. All great champions have a shield bearer go before them. Things always wither before they die. Time always proceeds Death.

If Mankind cannot slay time, how then can he contend with the light of death himself, the Widow Maker? He cannot even contend with the skin of his own flesh, which wastes away faster than anything known to man. It does not matter the age of the individual. For even the most advanced of age among men is but a speck of dust beneath the fingernail of time. Every second 100,000 cells die in the body. Its through the consumption of other dead things we eat and process as food. Those 100,000 new cells are born in their place.

Mankind created by the hand of God from the primal dust has a genetic connection to this world. Therefore, he naturally sets his heart on the temporality of it though it withers away. Be it the tangible things which the young covet like beauty and strength. They are but for a season. Be it the intangible things which old men seek and sacrifice all for like power and war, prestige and honor, glory, and dominance, it is all but for a season. It is said that the cold of the winter's night can make one long for the warmth of the summer's sun.

Mental frustration, isolation and abandonment were

all understatements in comparison to what Nevaeh had actually felt. She hoped for warmth and light. Right now, she only saw cold and darkness while she peeked out through the vent cover above the table in the break room. She waited quietly for the two lingering orderlies to leave. When they finally left, she swung the vent cover open, stuck her feet out and slowly dropped to the table. Her speech and appearance were harmonious. She whispered nastily to herself, "After all of the shit I've done to protect that psychotic bastard. Is this now how he rewards me by trying to kill me? I bloody swear the first chance I get I'll cut his fucking throat. If it's a fight he wants, then it's a fight he'll get."

Such vulgarity suggested that she was not a Baptist anymore. Her clothing suggested she was an outcast and no child of God. She glanced at her filthy reflection in the large, polished plaque of the serenity prayer. It was positioned next to a bulletin board of outdated in-house events. She paused and read its words. They appeared to mock her. Quickly she went and searched for any food left behind in the cupboard. She stuck her hand through the bottom of the vending machine and grabbed all the cakes, crackers, and candy bars she could get. She clawed desperately at one small bag of Cheetos until she broke a nail and left it behind. Next, she picked clean the top shelf in the refrigerator of a half-eaten sandwich, a brown banana, and some old pasta in a Tupperware bowl. Quickly she pulled her iPhone from her back pocket and searched for a signal. She whispered low to herself as her phone died from a low battery, "Shit! $1,100 for this phone and the battery is a piece of crap." She loaded everything into a discarded plastic bag in the garbage. She hopped back up on the table and pulled herself back into the vent. She closed the cover behind herself and began to crawl back through the maze of aqueducts to her temporary resting place. Though many external areas of the asylum appeared brand new with exquisite designs, the veined ventilation system was as old as the family burial lot that still marked the side of the house.

Nevaeh's personal appearance changed dramatically after she had crawled through roughly a mile of twists and turns. Decades of dust had slowly buried several decomposed shells of dead things in small spots throughout the system. Spots for small critters like rodents, squirrels, and bats. They thought would be a good safe haven against larger predators like racoons, boa constrictor snakes and Tasmanian devils looking for a quick meal. Most of these feral creatures met their demise when they foolishly trapped themselves into a corner, therefore they essentially killed themselves.

Nevaeh knew that when escaping her predator time was of the essence. She had to stay one step ahead of him. She pondered how all of this came to be. Events set in motion from the time that she and Dr. Rutowski first met. Though he recognized her extraordinary ability. Just one touch by the hand of time and all that she both naturally knew and learned to love in this world with himhad withered away. Her personal ambitions were gone, dramatically changed. She once envisioned her career growing and maybe even one day having a private practice of her own. Now she only thought about how she would survive the darkness that hunted her in the asylum. Her most intimate relationship with her mentor and friend was gone, destroyed over the course of time by the words of the book tucked into the waistline of her skirt. She once bore an internal hope she would never face this kind of struggle again, like she faced under forced labor in the Red-Light district of Amsterdam. While all hope quietly died in her a voice grew louder and louder in her that said, "You can't trust anyone."

Faint traces of light spotted the asylum's dirt caked aqueduct system. Most of these vents marked off staff offices, patient rooms, and general corridors. The reaming ones gave access to a janitor closet, main kitchen, staff breakroom, and front lobby above the security desk. Even though the circumstances that surrounded Nevaeh were dire she still possessed a distinct advantage over everyone else in the asylum. They were all captives of the Widow Maker in one form or another. However, the general population was confounded to the surface level of this asylum, with a psychopath, one that left no trace of their mentor, colleague or provider, Dr. Marcus Rutowski. Nevaeh, on the other hand, had a strategic advantage. She was temporarily removed from any direct threat from him.

She also had the ability to move about most of the main grounds virtually undetected. Plus, the ventilation system allowed her the advantage to eavesdrop from a safe cloaked position. When Nevaeh finally reached the systems hub three ventilation shafts intersected between the private wing of the main house, the staff administration wing, and the impatient wing of the asylum. There she lay down quietly and listened in all directions from the fork in the road. She cried softly until her paranoia decreased and she fell asleep.

Meanwhile, Dr. Rutowski spent the night in the chamber. The next morning, he restricted all movement through the main security gate to be cleared by him. That way he could be there to personally observe all traffic. The Widow Maker had grown most pleased when he looked at Dr. Rutowski through the looking glass of his mind. He had followed a talking rabbit down the hole into another realm. A realm that his former life experiences and training could not have possibly prepared him for. There he became like Alice under the demented guide of the Mad Hatter, who loved to see a pair of eyes roll loosely in a decapitated head. Dr. Rutowski was fascinated by the Widow Maker's odd rather insane behavior. Although there was something lost and very disturbed about him, he felt drawn and compelled beyond reason to continue on with him, that he may regain the journal and slay the empress of chaos, Nevaeh. She had stolen from them and daily worked to destroy the strange harmonic beauty in this desert wasteland, the asylum. Despite her efforts, the Widow Maker led Dr. Rutowski by the hand and nurtured all his thoughts. Over time he evolved beautifully far better in some ways than he had ever fathomed. Deception became his natural smile. When a majority of patients and staff looked into his eyes nothing existed. They saw not a trace of anything that would cause alarm or panic. However, to the three survivors that had witnessed the rarity of his flesh, Nevaeh, Emily, and Raquel. Each time one of them looked at him their eyes became cold as if somehow looking at him was like looking at Medusa and it caused a little bit of their soul to turn to stone inside. His eyes were not warm, soothing pools of psychiatric comfort. Rather they were scorched lakes of fire for torment. Their glass film deflected the world around him. He could not be persuaded in the least regard. Judgement was set in his dark heart. There was only the absence of light pure darkness. Darkness that birthed a mind created by an alignment of both exterior and interior factors gone violently wrong, the perfect storm.

Still, there are always some that seem to bear a keen sense of perceptibility in the midst of a storm. They become like lighthouses for the faint of heart around them. Their eyesight sharp as an eagle's. their minds as still as dust on the moon.

Nevaeh, Emily, and Raquel were the only exceptions that appeared tempered by this storm. Each of them had witnessed firsthand the cruel measures his dark side was capable of. They had stood under a grievous trial and suffered no physical scars. Mentally, they had been ravaged beyond the promised grip that any modern medication offered. There would be no appeasement or kiss from mankind. No total recall mind scrub chair that brevity could instantaneously create in them the mental fortitude of a monk. No hand-held neurological device to erase away days, weeks, months, or years that could take them back to the time before the darkness. He would always be with them. For once the Widow Maker had gained access to someone's life. He would always be there like sickle cell anemia. He became a trait in their flesh, a permanent staple in their mind.

Nevaeh awoke to the ventilated sound of a muffled plea at the end of one of the shafted corridors. Slowly, she sat up as her level of paranoia quickly increased. She quietly eased onto her hands and knees and leaned closer toward each direction until she discovered exactly which of the three shafts the muffled cry came out of. She paused briefly while she tried to figure out what was possibly down there and if it was moving towards her. It suddenly dawned on her that the noise had come from the main house, that more than likely it was a cry for help by one of the captive students Dr. Rutowski had locked away on the abandoned wing. The ventilation shaft was dark. Nevaeh strained to make out what was in front of her as she cautiously moved forward, down the shaft. She jumped and patted the darkness each time she put her hand forward. Terrified, she placed her hand on the next spot of cold metal in front of her. This was unchartered territory. She did not know what was in there, lived in there with her. When her fears fully overwhelmed her, she vomited a little in her mouth and almost jumped out of her skin. When she touched the tail of a dry brittle form. Maybe it was a possum? Perhaps a diseased cat whose fur coat was shedding? She tried to brush it aside, but the moisture from its decomposed body had dried. Now the corpse was stuck in that place. She had no choice except to crawl over it if she were to ever reach the room full of trapped college students over at the main house and help them escape.

CHAPTER 17
DRY COFFINS

N o one had seen Nevaeh in nearly two days and a
newly elected city official had scheduled a tour
of the facility with her personal assistant. This
could not have come at a worse time for Dr. Rutowski.
The first day a politician takes office always marked
a significant time of transition. Some immediately
fit the current mold engraved by dozens of others
before them. Some on the flip side of the coin tried to
brainwash their colleagues to believe the same lies that
they told their constituents. Old ideas that governed are
easily replaced. Until new ideas pose more of a threat
to norms and comforts than the old ones ever did. Not
knowing the official's intentions, Dr. Rutowski hoped
she would not be a problem. The Widow Maker on the
other hand, had hoped that she would be just that. He

grew increasingly restless as Nevaeh's scent waned in his nostrils. The hunt of new prey always scratched the itch he held in his mind.

Preparation of the day's itinerary demanded Dr. Rutowski immaculately dress. He wore a tailored made pair of black linen trousers with a fine silver cross stitch thread. His shirt a crisp white, with a small collar, a wide red tie, and a black suit vest. He had a conference room with a large viewing window specially prepared to impress her with. All in-house staff members were cleared to attend in ten-minute intervals for refreshments. No patients could attend for security purposes. White cake was promised to them if everyone played nicely during the visit.

Midway through the visit, Dr. Rutowski detected no problem firsthand, so he excused himself to go do a round, but actually went into the viewing room for further observation. The door had barely closed to the room when Dr. Rutowski began to hear the familiar chime of six nickels falling to the ground as his vision grew hazy. The Widow Maker whispered in his mind, "Can the Ethiopian change his skin or the leopard his spots?" Together they watched as the councilwoman's behavior immediately changed. She no longer appeared as an avid admirer. Now her eyes gleamed with suspicion. Her voice low and full of scrutiny. The Widow Maker smiled deathly at her through the tinted glass when she walked over to its' mirrored side. She boasted about her plans to modify the privatized contract with the city and bring in more oversight. That in her opinion no one man should have complete control over a project of this size.

Upon hearing that the dark intent of the Widow Maker multiplied against her. He immediately disappeared from the other side of the viewing window and appeared back at the conference room door. When neither the councilwoman or her assistant had noticed him re-enter the room, he navigated behind several staff members and added several droplets of a clear liquid to both of their glasses of apple cider. When he disappeared back into the crowd, they were none the wiser. The councilwoman picked up her drink and continued in a conversation. When her assistant went to get more juice, she was shocked to notice that Dr. Rutowski had returned to the room. At first, he seemed to pay her no mind at all. She looked away briefly to take a sip from her juice. When she looked back for him, he was gone and so was her assistant. She scanned the room for any trace of them and suddenly noticed that he was on the opposite side of the room. His gaze was fixed tightly on her. All she saw at first was what he wanted her to see. Namely his brightly polished teeth accosted by a warm angelic smile. The small crowd of staff parted for him as he approached her. It was then that she realized they were loyal only to him. They were his disciples and he, their messiah. She trembled and as she quickly thought about all that she had foolishly told them and tried to force a smile as he said, "Come with me councilwoman. There's a rare find, a muse if you will, here on the grounds, in my office that I want you to see." She sought an exit and replied, "Maybe next time. I have several other appointments I must tend to." She turned again to signal for her assistant and saw nothing but the small saucer of cake she had on the edge of the table by the door with her cup. When she looked back at him, she saw for the first time the darkness in his eyes that seemed to swallow the light. The Widow Maker lowered his gaze and said, "Now what kind of host would I be if you came all this way and I showed you no true treasure? I'm sure your assistant can manage to interview staff and learn about our patients in your absence."

Before she could answer the Widow Maker took the glass of apple cider from her hand and led her to the door. She could not help but notice on the way to his office that the hallways were quite empty. The report of this vibrant mental health facility in actuality felt like being in a dry coffin. Her throat grew drier with each passing moment. Suddenly, she felt restricted, unable to breathe, confounded within the itch of her own skin. Her balance began to give way. Her skin temperature began to boil so she placed her face against the cool surface of the wall. Through blurred vision, she raised a limp arm after him. Her thoughts grew increasingly confused. She thought they were close to his office, but now he appeared half a hallway's distance away. She wanted to turn back, but her body kept following him as if she had no control over it. When she reached his office, he had gone inside, and the door remained open. She said, "I'm feeling a little lightheaded. I think I should sit down." Then she collapsed in a square padded chair.

Dr. Rutowski pulled out his medical examiner's flashlight and checked her eyes. He said, "It appears that the sedative I gave you in the conference room is working nicely. Come into my private chamber. You can lie down there until we're ready to begin. Here, let me help you." While he moved the bookcase, she squinted at the thirteen white boxes, which seemed to exuberate light. Her vision faded out to nothingness as he lifted her like a rag doll and flung her over his shoulder and carried her down into the chamber. Thirty minutes later he emerged from his office alone, cleaning his hands with a rag. A passing staff member asked, "Sir, do you need anything?"

Dr. Rutowski replied, "No thanks, I'm fine. I was just tidying up a bit," and felt there was no need to return to the conference room. Instead, he headed over to the main security station in the front lobby. He went to collect the personal effect bags of the councilwoman and her personal assistant from the property counter. While there he looked over the entry logs and returned the two security clearance ID tags from the guests. Before he left, he overheard two security guards talking about a recent theft of petty items. The first guard said, "You know someone stole my half-eaten sandwich form the refrigerator in the breakroom two days ago.

Then they got my Pringles after that."

The second security guard replied, "Well, whoever it was it sure wasn't a patient that rummaged through the cabinets looking for food to eat. A patient wouldn't make it that far from the secure wing. Plus, if they did, why spend time bumping the vending machine to get snacks? Why not just try to get out? It doesn't fit to me."

Dr. Rutowski slowly walked away as he calculated that this first event happened about the time Nevaeh had disappeared. He pondered, if it was her, how did she get past security without being seen? Without delay he went to the breakroom to investigate. He inspected the cabinet and vending machine. Things were in complete disarray just as the guards had said. He noticed what looked like a fingernail in one of the bottom rows of the vending machine. So, he bought a packet of Spearmint bubble gum to push the nail from the circular slot. He retrieved the nail alongside the gum and analyzed it briefly. He noticed several thick dirt black fingerprints smudged across the push door of the vending machine. He squatted to examine the small smudges closer. Then his eyes trailed off from the dirt-streaked fingerprints to the vent above the breakroom table. He smiled and walked over to the imprint of a woman's small fingers leaving a trail through the missing dust headed inside the vent. Through gritted teeth he exclaimed, "Nevaeh!" Suddenly he began to hear the familiar chime of six nickels falling to the ground as his vision grew hazy.

The Widow Maker mumbled low before he turned to leave the room, "Nothing allures a young mouse like a fresh piece of cheese." Then it dawned on him, "I know what's better than one piece of cheese, five pieces of cheese." Then, he made his way over to the main house. When he arrived there and was about to enter the room that he held the five college students captive in. He heard hushed whispers come from inside. He paused and listened outside the door in hopes to discover a plot. Although he could not fully make out who the students were talking to, he assumed it was Nevaeh. Thirst consumed his thoughts, like a dry mouth longing for water, at the possibility of being close to the journal. When he could no longer contain it, he raced to open the door. He did not see Nevaeh but could smell her scent and knew that she was close by. He took a deep breath, removed his glasses from his pocket and began to polish them while he walked back and forth.

When he knew he had her attention he spoke softly, "Nevaeh, my child, listen to me. You were the first of many rare case studies. You've been with me far longer than any of these. I've found it astonishing that even with your rare ability to learn the micro expressions exhibited by others and readily display them back as a means to reestablish trust with them. Yet, you've failed to learn that being human is a condition that requires a little anesthesia called reality. Well, here's a dose of reality for you. You've been hoodwinked, blinded by your futile ambitions. There's not another soul on my hallowed grounds that would trade places with you. Why any one of them would trade your life in the blink of an eye for theirs. You can't trust someone that desperately needs something from you. I've never met a person who didn't need something. Right now, they need you to be their Tiger-Killer. The idiot that's sent out of the village to kill the tiger while everyone else hides.

Also, you're sadly mistaken if you think its only the living in this room that will judge you successful. If you somehow can stop me the Tiger and help them escape, that the dead will have nothing to say. I speak for the dead, and you will soon learn that the dead have far more to say. For although you are the one getting the test, all of you will live with the results. You will be mocked for all of eternity. When you walk along the shores of the nether world with no eyes or tongue. Many will say, 'Look over there. It's the fool that tested the Widow Maker, failed miserably and damned us all to this place.' For not one of them will receive a fee for the Boatman Charon to cross over the River Styx. However, you can put an end to all of this, and I will overlook your transgression. If not? I promise you, you'll only wish you had a dry coffin to seek refuge in. As a matter of fact, the clock starts now."

The Widow Maker turned swiftly and headed towards the huddled group. He said, "Come child, its not polite to keep the doctor waiting." Scared, the others clamored out of his way. Karen said, "Please, I have a family."

With a violent kick to Karen's skull, she was half conscious. Then the Widow Maker responded coldly, "Why does everyone keep telling me that?" He tortured Karen for hours in the room across the hall. It was far enough away so that other staff would not hear. It was close enough so that her screams would torture Nevaeh with the other four students. Nevaeh tried to cover her ears to drown out the sound, but Karen's scream shook the ventilation shaft. He gutted her like a fish and wrapped her small intestine around her neck like a scarf. Later that night he propped her up in a chair and pushed her back into the room with the others. Her face was ice blue. A note was tacked to the chest of her leather jacket that said, "It'll be a cold day in hell before I let any one of them leave this room alive. JUST GIVE US BACK THE JOURNAL!"

Time blurred over the next few days and Nevaeh remained in isolations. She also accepted the warm ventilation shaft as a final resting place. She spent the majority of her hours awake in perpetual fear, like a battered housewife. She felt a horrible vexation dominate her. All she had with her was the journal. Daily the darkness of its words called to her like a firefly into the night. Everybody she had spoken to lately was dead. The Widow Maker had turned her tranquil life upside down into a suicide hotline.

CHAPTER 18
EULOGY OF LIES

W hen a viper strikes, it leaves an enzyme that other vipers can smell. Inside the enzyme is a mental code that tells them the meal is safe. Emily knew Dr. Rutowski had struck fear into the hearts of every resident in the asylum. Carefully she sniffed about the ravaged mass in hopes to find someone, anyone that did not bear the scent of his enzyme. She had to regain her own personal strength. The rules of engagement had changed. It was never in Emily's plan to try to escape the asylum. Actually, it was quite the opposite. She envisioned the asylum being her personal playground. A place where an endless drove of mindless incompetence shuffled past her like an auction block of souls primed for the taking. Souls that had been stripped away from all that they knew.

That had lost families, homes and most dear to them access to their addictions. That was the lie they coveted most. Daily it fed them child-like delusions of grandeur, where every day was a sunny day.

However, for Emily none of that mattered. They were all, even her, destined for misery and pain. She eased her chair by the door of her room and surveyed the asylum's terrain. The specialized housing unit was designed for fourteen patients. The current body count sat only at five. She had trapped the sixth patient that remained in active status on the roster. He was till in isolation as far as she knew. Judging by the increasingly bloodthirsty behavior of Dr. Rutowski's psychosis his fate was sealed. There would be no redemption for him. At the time, Sam Green appeared a reasonable trade in the interest of maintaining her cloaked identity. She did not know what he would do with the information they had on her, so she decided not to take the chance. She thought it best to remove him from the picture rather than add another should have, would have, or could have to the treasure chest of her regrets. She smiled as the irony of the situation settled in. She still ended up making a deposit in that box. She had lied to herself and pretended that she did not need him. Now she wished he were there. The rest? They had been collected one by one like old Coca Cola bottle caps. While she sensed a terrible fate awaited her.

One name came to mind, "Prometheus." Greek mythology claimed that he had been strapped to a barren rock in the middle of the Adriatic Sea. Although close to water, he was slayed with thirst by the heat of the sun during the day. Then he was frozen by blasts of cold Arctic air during the night. A large raven came every morning from the valley and plucked out his eyes so he could not see. His eyes grew back every night only to have them plucked out again in the morning. Had Stonewall Asylum become Emily's barren rock in the middle of this Adriatic Sea called the Louisiana Bayou? The Widow Maker being the ravenous bird had come and taken her eyes daily. She lowered her head and laughed as she said, "After all these years of pretending to be intellectually challenged, I've finally lost my mind." When she lifted her head, Raquel was standing in the doorway of her room a little ways down the hall. Her eyes were and wide as bright as newly minted quarters. Although the hall was empty, she said loudly, "Can you help me with a puzzle I'm working on in m room?" Then she whispered lowly as she walked over to her, "Nevaeh asked me to come get you."

Emily responded, "I knew she hadn't left the asylum. Where is she now?"

A nosey patient eavesdropped from her doorway and asked, "Where's who?"

Raquel quickly said, "All of the staff that's supposed to be bringing us cake from the party they are throwing up front."

The nosey patient responded, "Aw, I want cake."

Emily glared at her and said, "Interrupt me again and

I'll personally deliver you cake."

The nosey patient asked, "What was that?"

Raquel interjected, "Nothing, she just said we'll be sure you get cake." Raquel closed her room door after she and Emily were inside.

Emily stated, "I thought you said Nevaeh wanted me. Where is she?"

Nevaeh said, "Psst, Emily, up here."

Emily slowly looked up at the vent above the dresser in Raquel's room. She barely made out Navaeh's eyes that hovered a ways back from the vent cover. Emily smiled and moved herself closer to the vent. Slowly she closed her eyes and listened to Nevaeh describe many things she had learned about Dr. Rutowski. She already knew most of what Nevaeh told her about his psychosis. She knew nothing about the 13 small white boxes on display in his office. She reluctantly told her about the journal she took from his office. She feared she would ask to see it. Emily dismissed the journal as nothing that would improve their current situation. She encouraged Nevaeh to hold onto it as all costs. That it had already brought all of them some much needed time, that in his eyes they were all on his list and therefore already dead. His only job was to give them a fee for the Boatman. The journal was indeed a key to achieve that. It was at the core or source of where he received his power. It would have been better if she had never touched it. Now that she had it, she could not just give it back. If he got it back all of their fates would be sealed. At least for now some of them stood a chance to make it out alive. Raquel signaled to Emily and Nevaeh that they had to hurry up before someone came. While they headed out the door, Nevaeh asked Emily, "Can I trust you?"

Emily said, "Just do your part. I'll be sure to do mine."

Nevaeh scooted back into the darkness.

When Raquel opened the door to her room Dr. Rutowski was at the corner of the hall. He stepped back and witnessed Raquel push Emily back to her room. He immediately thought that it was unusual that those two were together. They were polar opposites by nature, but now they moved together as if they were one. What had transpired in Raquel's room to the docile lamb? That now she appeared reborn like a phoenix from its ashes. She had spent 40 days and 40 nights trying to hide from darkness. She had been ripped apart by it, destroyed by it. Now she clearly comprehended what few ever do. The only way to truly see light is from a dark place. The grand scheme of things said that she was a pawn, the first mouse. The Widow Maker smiled as he forcibly placed her head in a trap so that he the second mouse could get the cheese.

Dr. Rutowski folded his arms across his chest and leaned flush against the wall. Alliances were being formed from extreme ends in his house. Given the asylum's current state of duress this spelled out pure desperation. They had pooled their resources to try to fulfill a common goal. That goal could only be one thing. They wanted out. Still with just the two of them it was not enough. Only one of them had ever left the secure patient wing. At that time, she was half unconscious and out of her mind. After her epiphany she traveled one corridor clutched to Nevaeh's arm and returned back here. So, what resources could she possibly provide? If they were truly to be profitable, they needed administrative help. Someone with intimate knowledge of the asylum's security systems.

He looked over his shoulder toward the echoed sound of something that moved inside the ventilation shaft. Suddenly he began to hear the familiar chime of six nickels falling to the ground as his vision grew hazy. His left hand emerged from his pocket as it twirled a highly polished nickel between his index finger, middle finger, and thumb. The Widow Maker looked up out the corner of his eye and said, "I know exactly what you two are thinking. Nevaeh won't be able to help you two. You, however, will help me trap her. She can't hide in the vents forever. Whenever she does emerge, she will come for you two and I'll sever her head the moment I lay eyes on her." Piercingly he looked at the vent cover while he walked off.

Camille and Teri covered Karen's dead body with their coats to try to show some respect. Meanwhile, Alexander and Ethan used the faint light in the room to examine the door. Alexander said, "This is pointless. The lock mechanism is on the other side of the door.

Plus, we have no tools to even try to remove these hinges."

Ethan snapped, "Look Alex, I get that part. What if we've been going about this all wrong?"

Alex said, "What do you mean?"

Ethan paced by the door as he said, "I think our problem is not how do we get through this door, but inside these walls. I'm willing to bet that a house this old has a large crawl space between the walls."

Alex walked over and kicked a wall. Even though he was weak, his foot almost went through. He looked over at Ethan and smiled. The girls stood and watched for several minutes while the two kicked a hole in the wall large enough for one person to fit through. Ethan squatted and stuck his head through the wall. A few faint beams of light filled with dust spotted the narrow corridor that disappeared into darkness. Ethan said, "It looks clear. Alright, Teri, we need you to crawl through and go get help."

Teri stepped back in fear and said, "Oh no, not me. Why do I have to go in there?"

Ethan said, "Teri, you're the only on that can fit. It took me and Alex five, almost ten minutes to kick this hole in the wall. Neither one of us have any more strength to widen it."

Teri looked at Camille as she spoke up, "Don't worry. You can do this." Teri swallowed slow and dryly. Her eyes bulged with fear. She stooped down, peeked inside. She froze when she saw the hallway disappear into darkness. The others urged her, so she climbed through. She cringed at several spider webs that she walked backwards into. She prayed to calm herself as she inched down the hall. The other three students whispered through the wall to her, "Teri, hurry, we don't have that much time!"

Teri walked heel to toe down the hall. She paused each time she reached a dust covered beam of light. Desperately she squinted and tried to look through it into the next room. She jumped at a mouse that scurried across her foot. She paused briefly to collect herself. When she looked up the welcome beams of light were gone. The hall was completely engulfed by darkness for about sixty feet. She dreaded to take another step. Three voices whispered down the hall from the three trapped students. Teri told herself, "I can do this. I'm almost there, just keep moving." She stretched out both of her hands in front of her and prayed all the more as she stepped into the darkness. About six feet in front of her a floorboard creaked. She grew ever silent and hoped she had imagined it. Then she heard a full weighted footstep. Someone was there with her. Fear absorbed the strength in her body. Her legs became tangled as she turned to flee, and she collapsed. The approach of footsteps multiplied in the corridor. Quickly they closed in on her. She slipped and fell twice as she scrambled to her feet. A strong hand grabbed her by the throat in the darkness and a hypodermic needle pierced her neck. She kicked the walls several times.

Meanwhile, Camille called out, "Teri, answer me. Teri?"

The heels of Teri's shoes scraped the floor as she was dragged deeper into the darkness. Moments later she awoke in the chamber. Her blurred vision slowly adjusted to the rusted twine wrapped around her chest. It secured her to an old whipping post at the center of the main room. She shook as she tried to scream. Dr. Rutowski jammed a red oil-soaked cloth in her mouth. Then she took several zip ties and pulled them tightly around each of her arms. This cut off her blood circulation. Soon, tiny electrical shocks filled her fingers behind numbness. Last, she injected her in the wrists with snake venom. A warm burn resonated as she used a rusted pairing knife to expose the skeletal bone in her hands. She peeled back the flesh past the second knuckle in each finger and rinsed her hand with warm water. Teri's eyes rolled in her head as the Widow Maker said, "I think your gender transformation has just taken a dramatic turn."

Teri pleaded as a plexiglass box with a thick rubber seal was set over her head and strapped tightly onto her neck. The Widow Maker filled the box wit ha murky, leach infested water and told her, "Haven't you heard? Life is not about the moments you breathe, but about the moments that take your breath away." At that moment, a seizure hit Teri. Several leeches swam up her nose and sealed off her airway.

Chapter 19
Pleading with Darkness

N evaeh stole two boxes of Rice Crispy cereal bars out of the kitchen and headed back through the ventilation system to the starved college students. When she finally arrived, she saw only three of them huddled together by one wall. Curious as to what they were doing, but still very excited about the alliance she had made with Raquel and Emily, she eased to the edge of the shaft and said, "Hey guys, I have some good news!"

Camille looked up at the vent. Unlike other times she did not appear glad to see Nevaeh. Nevaeh continued, "First, I brought food. Second, I got two others that are going to help us to get out of here."

No answer came in response to her jubilant news. Only the look of foolishness that covered their faces as the other two looked up. Nevaeh asked, "What did you do? Where's Teri?"

Ethan tried to explain, "It's been almost a day since we last saw you. We didn't know if he got you too?"

Nevaeh repeated, "What did you do?"

Alex cut in, "We thought it was our only chance to get out of here."

Nevaeh asked, "Where's Teri?"

Camille said, "She crawled through this hole in the wall over three hours ago. She went to get help and hasn't come back."

Nevaeh said, "You three come over here so I can talk to you. I have something very difficult to say."

Slowly Ethan, Alex, and Camille walked over and stood under the vent. Nevaeh told them dryly, "Our time has run out. We have 48 hours to get out of this place or we'll never leave here. Now I have someone who believes she can distract him long enough for me to get the spare set of skeleton keys I've already stashed in a bag I hid. We'll never get the key from around Dr. Rutowski's neck. Once I have those keys, we are going to gather as many patients as possible and get the hell out of this place."

Camille stuttered, "But wha . . wha . . what about Teri?"

Nevaeh went silent, then said plainly, "Teri's gone and don't either one of you try to go looking for her in those crawl spaces. If you do, you won't come back either. This is his house, and he knows it well. That's why I've spent the last five days living in this filthy ventilation system, sleeping in God knows what. I'm doing all I can to get us out of here. The best thing you can do now is pray he doesn't come for you. I'm going into the lion's den to try and draw his attention. Pray for me." She bent the two boxes of cereal bars and pushed them out through the small eighteen by six-inch vent once she kicked its cover off. Then she tunneled back through the ventilation system.

The city official's eyes flickered as she awakened inside a large cage between smaller ones that held ten-pound rats. The malnourished, hungry wolves in cages across from her became excited towards her being a potential meal when they saw her move. The hand of a woman that she identified by her clothing and believed to be that of her assistant came into view. She lay motionless like a stillborn child, on top of a gurney, underneath a blood-soaked sheet. Several large scorpions with severed legs filled the table in front of her. Dr. Rutowski walked over and extracted 100 cc's of venom from two of his spliced specimens as he spoke his dark parable to her: "The first day of life is much like the last, you come and go alone. Light shines through the doorway of darkness and who truly understands it? Of all the possible thresholds to cross you've been chosen for this one. Death, the ambassador of a dying world, waits as a willing escort to guide. Will is an illusion of the mind within the grand design of true life. Come, drink from the cup of destruction, it beckons all flesh."

The city official screamed at the top of her lungs, "LET ME OUT OF HERE RIGHT NOW!"

The Widow Maker thumped the syringe with his finer to check the venomous measurement. He turned toward her like he was in the middle of a lecture and said, "The secret hope of every parent is that their child will be born without blemish, mental defect or spot so they may thrive. You, on the other hand, appear as if you would eat your young to advance your career. I've arranged a small lesson to nurture you into motherhood." He dragged her from the cage as she fought forcefully to stay inside. She pleaded, "Wait, I have money and resources. I can help your cause." He laughed and said, "Let me be clear with you. there will be no bargain. I'm not influenced or swayed by the fickle sentiments that so many have fallen to. I especially loath remorse. Now hole your tongue as the Reaper walks over your grave. He strapped her in an archaic childbirth chair from the 1500's. Then he injected a little of the venom in three spots along her spine like an epidural administered during child labor. He took a rusted butcher's knife and split the flesh of her back open like a skilled surgeon. The cut exposed her spine from between her shoulder blades down the center of her back, to just above her tailbone. The scent of her wound was like freshly cut watermelon. At once a new litter of mice smelled it. It drove them crazy. Quickly they crawled from a cage that contained several 10-pound rats. Slowly they climbed up the chair and ate their way past the thick nerve endings that surrounded the councilwoman's vertebrae. She twitched with fear, her pulse quickened, and her eyes shook as she felt her heart pound in her chest. She grew nauseous when she felt the mice, that where like warm bean bags, nestle together in the warm bed of her stomach lining. She felt each of their tiny bites slightly as hot bile ran down her leg. She vomited within moments and went into cardiac arrest. She cried out, "Oh Jesus!"

The Widow Maker responded coldly, "Leave Him out of this. He has nothing to do with this place."

Panic filled the councilwoman's feverish body as her blood boiled behind the mixture of strong toxins in her system. She felt the movement of the mice slow at the same pace her heart did. When it shut down the movements of the mice stopped as well. There they died in the lining of her stomach from a lack of oxygen. Thick foam pooled in the corner of her mouth.

At the back of the room were several pig slop buckets of highly polished nickels. The Widow Maker walked over, counted out six nickels and viscously jammed three of them into each of her eyes as a fee for the Boatman Charon. He walked past the viewing stall of Chico Rivera. Unlike times before, he said nothing. Dr. Rutowski walked over to him, lifted his head, and watched it drop. He was dead and had been for about six hours. Mockingly, he spoke as he climbed the staircase back to his office, "Looks like I'll have to devote more of my time and attention to trapping Nevaeh."

Nevaeh dozed off as she watched Raquel through the vent in her room. That night she had a dream. Her Astro projected form drifted through the bed and fell through the other side that mirrored but was not the real world. She awoke in what appeared to be another form, an older form of her room. Quietly, she laid in bed until her eyesight adjusted. She thought at first she had hallucinated when she glanced at her form on the bed through what appeared an osmosis like mirror on the ceiling, the gateway back to her actual world. Her aerial reflection showed she was in transparent lingerie on this side of the portal on top of flowing silk sheets. Her throat was extremely parched. Slowly, she sat up to find water. The glass of water she saw on the nightstand made her gag. It was filled with putrid pond-like water. Though it looked condemned, the room she was in was hers. The walls were dirt caked. The furniture weather worn, grayed and outdated. Solid ceiling to floor curtains blew in place of the missing patio doors and over the missing window. Barefooted, she left the room. She sensed she was alone and somehow belonged there. This condemned version of the original Stonewall Plantation looked as if it had been long abandoned. She froze when she noticed a large picture of herself. It was the centerpiece above the main staircase. She wore eighteenth century clothing and appeared as the madam of the house. She marveled at the portrait as she stepped backwards onto the front porch.

Outside the sky was filled with magnificent stars

that shimmered like a crystal lake. There, beneath the majestic the field was a manicured lawn, marked by a small strawberry patch and a large, grafted half plum, half peach tree. Several abnormally large black crows walked back and forth in the gravel outside the main gate. Freshly washed sheets blew gently on a clothing line. Nevaeh walked to the edge of the porch. She closed her eyes and inhaled deeply the fresh scent of recently fallen rain. Quietly, she sat down. It had been a long time since she felt her soul experience such peace.

Suddenly a loud crack-like hammer against plywood sounded in the field. The sky clouded and a cold fog blew in quickly. It shrouded the entire field, then withdrew as if by vacuum to the sediment filled pond out back. When the fog was gone the opulent field had left too. It had been replaced by a rugged, heavily beaten field of dirt. Four highly polished black coffins sat where the tree and fruit once were. Nevaeh mumbled to herself, "What the fuck?" Slowly, she stood up and headed down the steps. When she started towards the coffins, she jumped at a loud sound that was like a hammer that split plywood. She heard a muffled voice soon after. Someone was trapped inside one of those coffins. Carefully, she approached. Her toes gripped each spot of coarse dirt like it was Velcro. She stopped dead in her tracks when she heard another loud rap against wood. It came from inside another coffin. The sound repeated even louder and echoed across the field. Suddenly it was followed by the repeated knocks of someone in each coffin.

Nevaeh stumbled backwards as the coffins shook. When she turned to run, she realized that she was no longer in front of the house. Her feet were inside the old family burial lot. There were old Confederate flags etched into several of the old broken headstones there. The large crows that were outside the main gate stopped walking and turned their heads in unison toward the small burial lot. Nevaeh looked to see what had grabbed the crow's attention. There was now a lone black coffin that sat above ground next to a fresh mound of dirt with a shovel in it. A loud banging, along with a muffled but familiar voice started in the coffin. Nevaeh moved closer to try to make out the voice. She was suddenly distracted by the sound of hard sole dress shoes that crunched the dirt behind her. A cold chill swept across her flesh and the fine hairs on the back of her neck stood up. The sound of the weighted footsteps from an approaching figure grew louder behind her. When she turned, she was immediately grabbed around the throat. The Widow Maker lifted her off of her feet and stared piercingly into her dark chocolate eyes. They bulged with fear as she struggled for air. Frailty was in her gasps as her feet dangled almost two feet from the ground. Ethan, Alexander, Camille, along with Raquel stood by zombified in front of the four coffins. The Widow Maker's eyes were emotionless, void of any empathy. They were empty glass reflections like those of a tiger. Cold eyes that depicted one dominant thought, "Kill every prey as quick as possible."

Neveah tried to loosen his grip as he dragged her with ease toward the open grave. When they neared the pit, he picked her up and choke slammed her onto the mound of dirt. She hit next to the shovel with a thud as if she had landed on bedrock. All of the wind was knocked out of her lungs. She faked unconsciousness to prevent further assault. Darkness eclipsed her small delicate frame. Then he walked up the mound a couple of steps, grabbed the shovel and tossed it next to the previously dug hole. While his back was turned, she scrambled to her feet and ran. She tripped clumsily and fell onto the coffin. She screamed when she saw herself with nickel slotted eyes and the Latin inscription, "Lux Ab Exitium Velle Venere," carved across her forehead by a surgical instrument.

Nevaeh awoke to her own screams in the ventilation shaft. While she took several deep breaths to calm her nerves and racing thoughts a weird sound registered in her hearing of what seemed to be a belt buckle that scraped the floor of the shaft. Something was moving towards her. Then she heard deep breathing, followed by the weighted bending of the metal floor. She held her breath as a dark disturbed voice said, "The first day of life is much like the last, you come and go alone. Light shines through the doorway of darkness and who truly understands it? Of all the possible thresholds to cross you've been chosen for this one. Death, the ambassador of a dying world, waits as a willing escort to guide. Will is an illusion of the mind in the grand design of true life. Come, drink from the cup of destruction it beckons all flesh."

Quickly, Nevaeh flipped over, and bear crawled away just as the hand of Dr. Rutowski almost grabbed her foot. She reached one point in the mazed structure that she had often avoided. It was about a 20-foot drop, like a laundry chute. With nowhere to go and her hunter inching closer, the metal of his belt buckle getting louder, she dropped headfirst down the chute. The shoot led to one place, The Chamber. Socked and horrified by what she saw as she scrambled to her feet, she said, "Is this what he's been doing when he disappears at night?"

Several clothing lines, marked by old wooden clothes pins bore soiled pieces of odd, shaped parchment-like paper. They each bore dark archaic cut letters in Latin written on the front and back side. The closer she drew, the clearer the paper became. She vomited as each revealed that it was not paper at all but was actually dried human skin. Suddenly the wolves that listened became excited, agitated. The Chamber stirred as if it was feeding time. The large rats screeched their claws chipped at their makeshift cages. The odor was atrocious and stomach turning. Neveah noticed a faint beam of light cast at the bottom of an old cobblestone staircase, and she ran to it.

CHAPTER 20
UNHEARD PETITION

Nevaeh fled the highly grotesque scenery and quickly climbed the uncharted staircase in front of her. She paused when she reached a heavy wooden handleless door. Even after she swung open the bookcase and emerged into Dr. Rutowski's office. The residual effects of the images below still burned steadily in her mind. The treacherous chatter of the caged 10-pound rats scratched at her ears. She shook her clothing when she thought she felt a long moist rat tail slither across her skin, just below the nape of her neck. She almost stripped on the spot. She felt relieved when she discovered that the suspected rat tail was nothing more than the twisted damp material tag from the collar of her thick cotton sweatshirt. When a shadowed figure covered the frosted window of the office door she squatted and hid below it. The image of the lone guard's hand that patrolled the hall lingered momentarily outside the window. He flashed his light inside, checked the doorknob, and then left. A minute later Nevaeh peaked out into the hall. When she took off in the opposite direction the guard had barely turned the corner. Barefooted, she ran back to the old wing of the main house. She smiled when she discovered her stash bag was still on the floor of an old storage closet. A putrid moisture had soaked into it from old mildew carpet that covered it. She rummaged through the bag and found the old set of skeleton keys that she had tucked away from the nightstand in her private quarters.

The heavy lever of the latch mechanism scraped stiffly several times and then turned over. When Ethan, Alex, and Camille heard the lever turn over and the door slowly pry open they huddled together. Nevaeh's hushed whisper was such a relief to them. Quietly she said, "Don't worry, it's just me guys." Then she ran over and hugged them tightly.

Camille sobbed as Nevaeh said, "Shhh, I know. Come on let's go."

While the students gathered their backpacks, Nevaeh noticed Karen's frame underneath several coats in the chair by the door. Slowly she walked toward her until Ethan dropped his bag. The loud thud caused Nevaeh to jump. Then she remembered a sadistic killer was close by and could be there at any moment. He would love nothing more than to make them permanent guests in his demented basement chamber. Nevaeh turned around as Ethan went to pick up his bag. She said, "Leave it. It will lonely slow us down. We've got to get to the lobby. Hurry!" She took them to the end of the hall and told them, "Take this hallway straight until you reach the kitchen. Cut through there and turn right when you come out. Go down to the end of the hallway and you'll be at the lobby."

Alex protested, "Nevaeh, come with us. What if we get lost?"

Nevaeh said, "I have to get the other patients. You can do this. Now get going. I'll meet you there in five minutes." Then she ran in the opposite direction. When she reached the corner of the hall, she pulled the fire alarm to signal Emily and Raquel. The sleeping security guard at the front desk jumped at the sound of the alarm. The sprinkler system was activated and all of the patients' doors automatically opened to aid in the fire evacuation. Since the asylum was located in a remote area away from modern emergency services another fail safe was designed to aid in the rapid response to preserve life. The security guard on duty had 10 minutes to reset the system, do a headcount, and answer the incoming dispatch call with a code.

When the fire alarm and sprinklers went off Sam was in bed. Quickly, he covered his head and said, "What the hell is going on?"

Meanwhile, Emily and Raquel gathered the other patients on the wing and headed to the sliding security door. When the guard appeared there, he said, "Stay calm and follow me. There's no need to panic. It will be over soon enough." When they reached the security desk in the main hall no one else was there. The guard reset the alarm and the sprinkler system. Then he said, "Wait here for me by my desk. I have to do a quick walk through and a headcount." When he left Nevaeh stepped from behind a heavy set of drapes that covered cracked, barred windows. They were all glad to see her. She said, "When I reached the wing it was empty, so I came here. Where is Ethan, Alex, and Camille?"

Completely lost and soaked in the maze of hallways, Camille whispered to Ethan and Alex, "We should have been at the lobby by now. I told you it was a right turn when we came out of the kitchen, not a left."

Alex tapped Ethan on the shoulder and said, "Look, it's the door to the room we were in. we've just went in a complete circle."

Ethan said, "Shit man! We're never going to get out of this place."

Camille leaned against the hall by a closed closet door and said, "Hey guys, I think we should just double back the way we came, find the kitchen and take a right turn. We can still make it. We need to hurry. Nevaeh can't wait for us forever."

The knob on the door slowly started to turn. Ethan said, "Come on guys, let's find that kitchen."

Camille left the wall as the two boys started down the hall. Suddenly the closet door opened. The Widow

Maker covered her mouth, pulled her inside the closet and quietly closed the door. When the two boys turned the corner Alex said, "Camille, I think that's the entryway to the kitchen down there on the right." When she did not answer they both looked back and saw no one. Quickly they ran back to the corner. The other hall was empty too. Nevaeh called from behind them, "Hey, guys, come on." That's the wrong way. I told you turn right. Where is Camille?"

Alex said, "She was just right here."

Nevaeh asked, "What happened?"

Ethan said, "I got confused with your directions and we turned left when we came out of the kitchen. We found ourselves back by the room we were in. we decided to find our way back to the kitchen. That's when she disappeared."

Nevaeh said, "Where were you when you last saw her?"

Alex said, "We were halfway down this other hall."

Nevaeh ran past them to the corner and looked down the hall. Once she saw the closet door she slowed, then stopped.

Ethan asked, "What is it?"

Nevaeh shushed him as she tiptoed closer. Suddenly the doorknob started to turn as she heard a weighted footstep come from behind the door. She waved the boys off behind her. The door cracked and she saw his eyes flicker like two pieces of coal in a mine. The door cracked a little more as she held her breath for fear and inched backwards on her toes. When she took another step back and turned to run, the door widened. The Widow Maker smiled deathly at her. His pearl white molars glistened in the corner of her eyes as she yelled, "Run!"

The slow echoed stride of his hard soled dress shoes resonated over the fast slaps of her barefooted pace. She slipped and fell twice as she clumsily turned the corner. The two boys high tailed it down the hall. When she arose to her feet, somehow, he was right over her. Nevaeh's eyes widened in fear as he reached out to grab her. She was very fortunate to scramble away from his powerful grip and demented gaze. The night security guard appeared at the end of the hallway as Nevaeh ran in that direction. Her lungs shook with fear as she screamed, "Help!"

The guard responded, "Ms Sharai, is that you?" He grabbed her by the shoulders and asked, "My God, what happened to you?"

Frantic, she cowered behind him and said, "He's coming!"

Dr. Rutowski turned the corner and said, "Breaking news, water is wet."

The guard looked up as a hungry drool covered his mouth like a lion. Rage filled his eyes like a madman protecting his dwelling. He said nothing as he approached, but slowly slipped his hand under his white lab coat. The guard asked, "Dr. Rutowski, is everything okay sir?"

When he was within arms reach Dr. Rutowski quickly pulled the first blade from the small of his back and thrust it deep into the guard's chest. He smiled as he looked over the guard's shoulder and into Nevaeh's eyes. Then slowly, he lifted him off of his feet and stared at him while thick blood poured from the corner of his mouth. Nevaeh spun around and pushed the two boys toward the lobby. Halfway down the hall she yelled over her shoulder, "Leave us alone you monster!"

Dr. Rutowski said, "Oh, the monster's coming." Suddenly, his body contorted violently as he yelled, "Rah!" Then, he began to hear the familiar chime of six nickels falling to the ground as his vision grew hazy. The Widow Maker slowly said, "There you are my busy little bee. I believe you have something that belongs to me. How about you go fix a set of chamomile tea? Fetch my journal and I won't kill you along with everybody else in this asylum." Terrified by his transformation she said nothing and ran. He glared at her and said, "Fine, have it y our way then."

When they reached the lobby, Emily was in her wheelchair next to the security desk. Raquel had already held up a heavy window for a long time. While the other three patients squeezed through the security bars. Nevaeh knew her arms were tired, so she quickly took her place. One patient got stuck. Ethan hurried to get Emily. The Widow Maker came out of nowhere and slammed his head on the desk. When Nevaeh heard the loud crash on the desktop, she looked over her shoulder and into the eyes of the Light of Death. He picked Ethan up above his head and told him, "Call to her boy or I will bathe in your sufferings."

Dazed, with a gash in his forehead, Ethan called out in a dry voice, "Nevaeh, please just give him back the journal."

Nevaeh whispered, "Ethan, you know I can't do that."

The Widow Maker tightened Ethan's collar and said, "I'm going to make a living pendant out of this one so I can hear his screams daily." Then he viscously snapped Ethan's spine across a bended knee. He glanced down at Emily and said, "I'll deal with you in a minute."

Ethan stretched his fingers toward Nevaeh and dryly whispered, "Help me."

Nevaeh pushed the last patient through that was partly stuck between the bars of the window. The heavy window lowered on her neck as she tried to get through herself. She struggled to lift it and then it closed a second time on her leg. She knew that she would not make it. While she hurried to get out the window it dropped again. She grimaced as it crushed her ankle. She had barely pulled her foot out by the time the Widow Maker made it to the window. She limped behind several drapes, knocked over a plant pot and went down the hall.

Ethan raised a limp hand after her and said, "Nevaeh, please!"

When Nevaeh stopped and looked back the Widow

Maker said, "Do something worthwhile with what's left of your meaningless life. I'll trade you him for the journal."

When Nevaeh pulled the journal from the waistline of her skirt and held it up his eyes widened. She taunted him, "Are you talking about this book?"

Aggressively he said, "Give me that!"

Nevaeh whispered toward Ethan, "I'm sorry, I can't. If I give it to him all of the others would have died for nothing." Then she ran off.

The Widow Maker yelled after her, "Give me that journal!" She disappeared around the corner.

The Widow Maker grabbed Ethan by the leg and said, "Let's move this discussion to a more comfortable environment."

Nevaeh made several attempts at climbing back into the ventilation shaft, but her ankle prevented her. She cowered in the dark corner of a musty closet behind some old carpet and cried.

Meanwhile, Raquel and the others stared at Emily through the heavy window. She was trapped inside with no one to open it. Nevaeh's' words instantly came to Raquel's memory, "Let me be honest. I don't think everyone will make it out."

Emily rolled to the window and examined it. The patients outside were shocked when she stood gracefully and tried to lift it. After several attempts and not even a budge, she slowly sat back down and smiled dementedly. She knew her fate like the window had been sealed. Raquel's eyes sadden for her condition, but still pointed at the guard booth. She needed Emily to press the button on the control panel at the same time she pressed the button in the security booth so that the main gate would open. Emily turned her head in bitterness. Raquel pleaded through the window. Emily relented, pointed at the booth, and rolled back to the control counter.

Downstairs in The Chamber, the Widow Maker chained Ethan to the floor. He placed the braid from his ponytail in a crank vice welded to a table. He cranked the vice until it pulled the hair and flesh from his scalp in once piece. He gave him a shot of hydrochloric acid through the back of his exposed head and watched his grayish brain matter bubble. Then he deposited six nickels into his eyes and dragged his body into the corner of the cell next to an emancipated patient. She cradled a pair of nurses' shoes to her chest as if they were a small child. The Widow Maker said, "I've brought you a guest." She made a gesture with her hands as if to say, 'he's not going to try to get my shoes, is he?'

The Widow Maker replied mockingly, "No, not Ethan. I'm afraid though he won't be too talkative. You see, he's got an awful lot on his mind. You see, he's a little upset that someone he trusted didn't hear his petition."

CHAPTER 21
PURIFICATION

There are dark corners that lay in every man's heart. Corners so dark that even the brightest, scarlet fire appears like cindered ash that floats in the night. It is said that darkness cannot be purified. It can only be destroyed by light when the secrets of men are revealed. Light takes all the power from darkness. Nevaeh had learned many dark secrets of Dr. Rutowski. She hoped that if she exposed them, it would put an end to his madness and somehow purify the asylum. She knew her only way to survive was to keep moving on the personal wing of the main house with its many hidden passageways. Passageways that Dr. Rutowski knew like the back of his hand. It was just a matter of time before he caught up with her.

So, to increase her chances of survival she headed over

to the administrative wing. A place where she believed it would be the last place that he would look for her. Cautiously, she tiptoed into the main conference room. This multipurpose room was utilized to discuss group itineraries, in-house problems, distressed behaviors, and changes in the overall treatment approach. It would be another four hours before any regular treatment, kitchen or janitorial staff arrived. For now, it was only her and Dr. Rutowski. Since she could not get out, she needed to stay alive until someone arrived. She had more than enough evidence to support her claims of his psychotic deterioration. She had the patient's eyewitness account of him killing the security guard and what he did to Alexander. That, coupled with the fact she still had the record of all his torturous, methodical, slayings continued in his personal journal, was plenty. She quickly checked the windows in the air-conditioned room and found that none of them opened. There were still party decorations and leftovers in the room, though.

Nevaeh quickly hunched under the table like a forgotten child in the jungle. She devoured some of the thick icing left on a cardboard cake tray in the garbage, along with a few half-eaten cookies. Then she took a candle lighter from the table. As she left, she noticed Sam Green's name on the whiteboard. He had been reassigned to a no-access padded room at the end of the hall. While she headed towards the room and hoped he was still alive.

Suddenly, the Widow Maker walked out of an office

and blocked her path. Nevaeh froze instantly. They eyed each other for several seconds. Then she said, "I know you're not Dr. Rutowski. Who are you?"

The Widow Maker seethed through his teeth, "Who am I, but desolation in the flesh. Come and drink from the chalice of destruction." The sound of his hard soled dress shoes filled the hall though he had not moved an inch. The Latin inscription "Lux Ab Exitium Velle Venere" reverberated off the walls as if from within an abys. Slowly he started towards her. While she ran the opposite way, she passed by a fire extinguisher. She grabbed it and broke out a window at the end of the hall. She tried to squeeze between the bars, but her chest barely made it through. Nevaeh pulled the candle lighter from her waist, yelled, "Go to hell!" Then she lit the drapes and ran. She went into the kitchen and hid in the cupboard. When she heard his footsteps come and go, she tried to quietly tiptoe out, but knocked a pot off the counter. Quickly he returned for another look. Enraged, he left after he tore the cupboards apart, but found no one.

A large hog laid on the table in the back butcher's area just beyond the swing door from the main kitchen. The sound of a lighter, then a glow appeared inside the belly of the hog. Then, a pairing knife cut a small hole in its side and Nevaeh's eye peeked out for safety. Suddenly the eye of the Widow Maker snapped back in front of her, and she screamed from inside the hog. With one swing of a meat cleaver into the belly of the beast Nevaeh became silent.

Nine days in isolation had heightened Sam Green's senses. He once heard everything. Now he heard nothing. No one came to get him when the fire alarm sounded half an hour ago and now, he smelled smoke. The sprinklers had come on for a while, but now they were off. Something was terribly wrong out there and he was trapped inside a padded coffin. The strong scent of fumes from burning wood, steel, mud, and paint seeped under the door. He had survived several deadly incursions on foreign soil and was damned if he would die in this rat trap. He beat heavily upon the thick padded walls and door in hopes someone would hear him. His loud slaps from inside the room were like the mere whispers of toddlers that played patty cake on the other side of the door. Sam's adrenaline-lit eyes filled the small observation window on the door. He realized soon that no one was coming for him, let alone even coming by. He knew that unless he found a way to escape this white box it would become his final resting place. He used his teeth to chew a hole through the thick cotton material that surrounded the door. When he finally had exposed enough of the stapled boarder under the cloth at the edge of the door, he quickly concentrated on tearing it from one staple at a time. When he got two fingers into the opening he yanked and pulled the cloth from around the door until the full frame was exposed. With all of the lock mechanisms in plain sight he had the door opened in a matter of seconds.

The hall was engulfed in flames. Sam draped a large portion of the heavy pad over himself as a protective covering. He tried to navigate the hall, but the flames were too intense. He kicked open several doors to try to find a point of escape. At the end of the hall, he found a full support handicap bathroom. He had barely made it inside when the flames engulfed the door. Quickly he pushed the door closed, jumped in the tub, and filled it with water.

While the flames spread toward the tub Sam took a deep breath and slowly laid down under the water. Tiny, controlled air bubbles drifted upwards from his nose periodically as the waters overflowed from the tub. The waters created a moist barrier that temporarily stayed off the deadly flames. Sam stared up through the waters at the ceiling and thought about his special op's submersion training. While the flames slowly crawled up the side of the porcelain tub like a kettle. Sam came up again for air. Suddenly, a slab of drywall fell like a cover on the tub and sealed it like the lid on a coffin.

Since there were no security guards to verify a false alarm at the asylum the fire department was dispatched to ensure the safety of all persons on the grounds. Then investigate the emergency response call. The ride to Stonewall asylum took the fire department about thirty-five minutes. During that time, the fire spread throughout the complex. While the small deployment of trucks worked over tow hours to put the massive fire out, flammable gas and liquids fueled the fire. This engulfed the first floor with intense flames.

Thick smoke filled the main lobby like a funnel cloud. Emily still sat at the desk in her wheelchair, smack dead in the center of it. A heavy oak beam crackled in several places as it collapsed and blocked the doorway. Emily coughed as she placed her hand over her mouth. Smoke burned her eyes as she dug blindly into the pocket of her house coat for pills. She emptied the entire bottle of trazadone into her mouth. Her face tightened with displeasure at the horrible taste of the sedative. Still, she chewed the tiny pills while she desperately hoped they would take effect quickly so that she could pass out from an overdose and die on her own terms. Within four minutes her vision dulled. Her fingertips went numb as she felt all the strength leave her body. One by one periodic brightly blurred images passed in front of her minds eye. With each slowed beat of her heart the images changed. "Bump, bump," she was five years old, and her mother happily chased her through sun dried laundry sheets that hung on the clothing line in back of their house. "Bump, bump" she was almost eleven years old, and she peeked through the keyhole of her bedroom door. Her drunken mother cried as she lay half naked on the couch. "Bump, bump" she was seventeen years old and patted the shovel spade on the dirt after she had just buried her mother alive. She heard a small bell slowly ring that matched the dying beat of her heart. Fire spread across the floor and up the side of her wheelchair as she lost consciousness. She did not flinch when the flannel house coat caught fire.

The sound of the firefighters' axes that struck the door rang out in the lobby. When the door was finally breached Emily Frost's corpse burned brightly like a Viking funeral in her wheelchair. The aftermath of the fire left the historic grounds in complete and utter ruins for as far as the eye could see. The foundational soil underneath the asylum had been heated to such a degree by the metal that it resulted in several partial landslides spread across several locations on the grounds. One of the areas of the asylum that suffered a complete collapse of structural integrity was Dr. Rutowski's office. The entire first floor corner was gone. It had been ripped from the side of the building like fermenting wine rips through old wineskins. Quickly taken as if by a sink hole in the state of Florida. The original foundation stones created a small pocket of air, which allowed the wolves to survive. They eventually chewed and bent their cages enough to separate them from the wall. They burrowed out through the damp soil from under several wooden beams and escaped. They emerged covered in mud with dark yellow eyes. When they ran into the field, they had the appearance of malnourished hellhounds.

Next, the unknown patient burrowed out behind the wolves. Barefoot in a soiled gown she followed them into the woods for food. Softly she brushed off the white shoes on her chest. There was no sign of Dr. Rutowski. All traces of the atrocities that had been rendered by the hand of the Widow Maker were gone. Any evidence of his live gallery buried deep like a tick into the obscure past of the cursed Stonewall grounds.

A burned wheelchair sat by what used to be the security station in the front lobby. Its seat held the charred remains of Emily Frost, the Downs Syndrome Killer. Water sprayed everywhere from several busted pipes in the walls. Emergency service personnel from multiple departments spread out thinly and scoured the grounds. They diligently looked for any signs of additional survivors that they hoped to add to the few patients that huddled by the front gate. After public records revealed that there should have been at least seventeen souls that stood in the driveway. Multiple fires burned and threatened progress. Partly standing walls and framework collapsed without a moment's notice. Still the search party courageously continued to look.

A wet set of fingers eased from beneath a slab of drywall and slid it back from across the top of a bathtub. Sam Green choked several times as he surfaced out of his watery grave and gasped for fresh air. His eyes looked around wildly in high alert. He expected to see a fire. All he saw was a partially standing structure of fragmented blackened rooms with missing doors, missing windows and walls that crumbled instantly when the wind blew against them. The floor had collapsed not far from him. Only two support breams remained above. He saw clearly where the sheet of drywall had fallen from that saved his life. A pile of muddied staff uniforms and soiled towels littered the room floor across the hall. Suddenly, he heard dogs bark, whistles blow, and people call out, "Hello, is anybody out there?"

Several searchlights spread out across fifty yards approached from the distance. Sam quickly climbed out of the tub and prepared to run. He leaped over the missing floor in the hall and into the laundry room. Although he stood a good chance of evading the search party, he did not have enough time to put enough distance between them and himself to hide his scent from the dogs. A quick glance at the burned remains of Emily Frost in her chair merited sympathy. It also made him remember her skilled performances. Sam whispered toward Emily, "Thanks for all that you've taught me. I hope that you rest in peace." He sifted through the mixed pile of clothes and quickly changed into a staff uniform. He pulled a few loose planks over himself and moaned, "Can you help me?" until the search party discovered him.

While the search party helped Sam to the driveway where the other patients that survived were at, the dogs began to sniff anxiously in the area where the wolves had crawled out of from beneath Dr. Rutowski's office. The ground began to shake as the staircase to the Chamber buckled. The bookshelf toppled and buried the entrance. Volunteer firefighters quickly pulled their dogs away as an ocean of loose soil slid across the foundation and quickly filled the holes' secret passageway like a cement truck.

Epilogue
Mailed Memories

———◦◯⌒◯◦———

His size 15, Frankenstein-like boot, pressed the rusted clutch inside the old 1940's style truck. The thick rubber sole of the boot made up for a four-inch difference of length from that of his other leg. His charred skin grafted hand struggled to grip and move the truck's old stick shift. Slowly the oil-based motor wined to catch gear as it made its way across the long, private road to Stonewall Asylum. A low-level dense fog rested there on the ground, just beyond its gates. All of its outer beauty had been burned away. It's exquisite exterior mask completely gone. It had been removed like old makeup that was no longer fit to hide a hideous scar.

Amongst the ruins of smoldered support beams. Scorched furniture and doorframes to missing rooms walked a dark figure. He wore all white from head to toe that consisted of a fedora style brim, crisp button-down dress shirt, creased dress slacks and hard soled dress shoes. His skin had been horribly burned as if struck by a passing bolt of lightning. When the door of the truck opened one of the driver's hands clasped the roof. Then the other hand emerged and held onto the door for balance. Burdensome, he placed his first boot onto the ground. When he stood up, he towered above the truck. His brittle knees buckled when he straightened his malnourished six foot, seven-inch-tall frame. His heavy overalls sagged and swung loosely as he walked stiffly over to a highly polished mailbox and deposited a package. The package had been wrapped in a brown wax-like butcher's paper then tied loosely with a thin coarse rope like freshly cut meat. The tall thin man looked cockeyed across the ruins of Stonewall Asylum. His left glass eye twisted partly upward when he blew his nose with a crusted rag then stuffed it back into his back pocket. When he sat down the truck dipped significantly to the ground on the driver's side.

Dr. Rutowski approached as the old motor cranked. He studied the truck carefully as it rocked and swayed. While it slowly turned around and made its way back down the long private road. He retrieved the package from the mailbox, paused and looked around. Then he went back inside the grounds. Although the front gate stood alone without any walls he tightly closed and locked it behind him. He eyed the package suspiciously as he walked over and snatched the charred remains of Emily Frost, the Downs Syndrome Killer, out of her wheelchair. He opened the flap of an old satchel that sat on the ground next to the wheelchair. He removed a Walkman cassette player from inside it and turned the tape over. He placed the headphones over his ears and pressed play.

Slowly, he swayed as he stood there with his eyes closed and became lost in the conceptually blended, dark symphonic, Beethoven like music of the Widow Maker. He sat down in Emily Frost's wheelchair, opened the recently delivered package and noticed that there was a book inside. Its cover was made from thick cuts of dried skin, sown crookedly together with a thread that had been dipped in blood. When he turned the book over, he immediately began to hear the familiar chime of six nickels falling to the ground as his vision grew hazy. Slowly he read the book's title out loud, "Blood of My Father." His nostrils flared as he smiled with contempt. Electrical flashes of light filled his eyes like that of an Aurora Borealis. Each of his pupils split in two and revealed a smaller set in each outer corner of his eyes. Enraged the Widow Maker seethed through his teeth, "Lux Ab Exitium Velle Venere." Then he stood and walked into the blinding sunlight.

ABOUT THE AUTHOR

Zoez Lajoune was born in Wauwatosa, Wisconsin. He studied creative writing at the College of St. Scholastica in Duluth Minnesota, under Dr. Zelman. He now lives in Coleraine, Minnesota.

Watch for Book 5 of The Widow Maker series:
The Widow Maker's Wife.

Coming Soon.

Sneak Peak

Book 5 of The Widow Maker Series
The Widow Maker's Wife

THE FRAY

The rustic concave pit was scarred by rough, porous, artless walls. It had long been abandoned by any thought of change, elegance or refinement. Painfully it sat unpolished in isolation, made with intentionality at the conception of the University of Minnesota's blood soaked foundation in 1851.

A time when early settlers massacred 100s of Native Americans for a barren flatland. All for mere convenience to simply construct a school. A building of which the ecology was designed to cultivate. The clearest perception of the most savage thoughts ever conceived and justified by mankind.

Those that sat there in attendance under Williamson Hall were primarily undergraduate students. Eager young minds that sought to become forensic examiners, criminal pathologists and Quantico statistical analysts. A small group of botanists were also present as part of their graduate studies. Which required they learn to detect meticulous signs of decomposition of various biological organisms. Signs that may be foreign to environments such as grasslands, forestries and coral reefs. A very necessary skill to determine if a corpse originated there or was moved from another location.

A panel of five armed professionals stood in a military style rank on stage to lecture. Penelope Cruz (Data Analyst) Agent Raj Sarkozy (Criminal Pathologist) Michelle Atlas (Financial Forensics) Kent Jones (Toxicology/Logistics) and Detective Tommy Soprano (Deviant Subgroups). The students were awestruck at the speed in which the panelists congealed. They instantly became knit together in thought liken woven fingers on a glove.

Though each person stood behind an individual podium. They spoke and moved flawlessly from topic to topic in unison. Seemingly effortlessly, they demonstrated like a sentient collective. The complex thought that goes into a high profile criminal investigation. The student body sat on the edge of their seats. They were captivated by the display of in depth knowledge across trails of bread crumbs connected to anatomy, toxicology, forensics, psychology and habituality.

Investigators are taught to approach their job with a coin of duality. It is equally important they understand the mind of their partner as much as they would a suspect. Daily somewhere between the two their life hung in the balance.

The other four panelists sensed that Det. Soprano

had grown tired of cinematic movie questions. He had more time on the force than all the others combined on the stage, 39 yrs in all. Though each workd in state, they were in his backyard. He intended to seize this liberty and snatch the covers off of the darkness that had swept into the Twin Cities. This wasn't the first time these fice decorated professionals had been together. They'd been successful on several joint task forces, except for one.

The Widow Maker slayings had left them all stumped. Det. Soprano and Agent Sarkozy had since retired. The others, by request, were placed on active desk duty. Not one of them was left untouched. Equally it had destroyed all of their pubic images and taken with it a piece of their souls.

Since that time no peace followed Det. Soprano. At night The Widow Maker's sadistic eyes watched him. They hovered in darkness on the other side of the cracked closet door. The Widow Maker had killed his marriage and forced him into retirement, just months before his fortieth year. Some say that it changed him, consumed him and still was with him. That's why he unknowingly drifted toward it in thought, and eventually conversation.

Det. Soprano stepped forward from behind the pdium to the edge of the stage. The others followed. He said "Having looked at the psychological make up of some of the most violent minds in recent Minnesota state history, like Carol MacIntyre and Dr. Marcus

Rutowski. You can see why it is necessary to learn the specialized training offered here at the UofM. So that you're prepared for real investigations. One's that won't tie up with nice little bows in a couple of days but remain active for years.

Active case log nation wide on average there are about 200 serial killers each year. That kill for pure revenge, visual fixation and mental release. 13 of them will become prolific in killing just for the hunt without the slightest thought of aftermath."

Agent Sarkozy stepped forward and said "Aftermath . . in a criminal investigation it symbolizes the horrific result of what abides after everything has been savagely cut down indiscriminately without any thought of the future. There are scores of families and communities that have suffered tremendously in the wake of the fray on the projector screen behind me."

Penelope Cruz said "Here's an unlikely individual that fits perfectly into the fray. Duye to the fact that this is still an active investigation we are prohibited from disclosing certain details. Active case file number 13418-041 Maria MacIntyre The Widow Maker's Wife. A seductively beautiful but destructive and beguiling woman. Her first victim was here in Rosemont Minnesota. There she harvested a man like a deer."

Kent Jones said "The last time she was seen was at the county morgue. She had faked her death with a shot of Tetrotetoxcin B. Which slows the heart to a beat per minute. When she left the morgue she hung her toe tag on the light switch. She likely obtained the medication from her husband's torture bag. Which he got with Resident Nurse Trainer Carmen MacIntyre's ID card, his mom, she had access to the medical supply room at Regions Hospital, in St. Paul. After that, like a desert mirage 'he was gone."

Michelle Atlas said "Meanwhile in his absence the woman of the house Maria MacIntyre began to collect her own pound of flesh. Financial records indicated she became obsessed with occult based books. This interest likely grew from her innermost demon, Madam Sinclair. She evolved to dominate her thoughts. Her words became much like the Bible. The sole word for Maria to live by. However in this book there were no words of comfort, no measures of grace and no forms of salvation. There was only bind, torture and kill.

THE GOD COMPLEX

CPSIA information can be obtained
at www.ICGtesting.com
Printed in the USA
BVHW031121300922
648381BV00013B/389